THE NEW QUEEN RISES

THE NEW QUEEN RISES

METAMORPHOSIS ONLINE™ BOOK TWO

NATALIE GREY

MICHAEL ANDERLE

From Natalie

For M and T

From Michael

*To Family, Friends and
Those Who Love
To Read.
May We All Enjoy Grace
To Live The Life We Are
Called.*

Gracie watched, dumbstruck, as her friend touched a finger to his lips. Not half an hour into the game and the effort with her band had already gone sideways.

"Man, I don't know." Chowder spun around slowly, muscles rippling beneath his gray-green skin. He looked over his shoulder and into the mirror before sticking his butt out and bending over to touch his toes, his back arched.

When he came up, he ran his hands through his thinning hair and then dropped his head back, striking a pose with his chest stuck out.

"Be honest, guys. Does this tabard make my ass look big?"

Gracie dropped her face into her hands and shook with helpless laughter.

Their team, fresh off the decision to start a formal guild, had decided to make their tabards together. It had been a unanimous vote to have Chowder model it while they chose, the Ocru male being best described as "gloriously ugly," and he was hamming it up big time.

For instance, at this particular moment, he was wearing nothing *but* the tabard.

"I'm going to have to be the voice of reason here," Kevin stated, his voice coming through the filters as a squeaky female Piskie.

His character crossed her tiny arms and tapped one foot. She was dwarfed by Chowder…and by everyone else, up to and including her amarok, the ice-demon wolf that was her current companion.

Kevin's character looked at Gracie. "We can't expect one tabard to suit all of us. It's the bridesmaids' dresses problem. Everyone needs a different cut."

"For instance," Alex quipped, pointing at the Piskie, "*you* could wear a handkerchief." His character was lurking in the corner with his bow slung over his back, a purple-furred panther at his side.

"That'll be just about enough out of you, Muscles McGee," Kevin told him severely. "Don't you think those biceps make you look a little bulky, honey?"

Alex did a flex emote. "Muscle sliders all the way up, baby."

"Does *anyone*," Gracie interjected in a long-suffering voice, "want to offer any input on the actual tabard?"

Chaos ensued.

"No."

"Nope."

"I think it should have a vomiting skull sigil."

"We said no to that already."

"Just thought someone might have changed their mind."

"Not in a million years."

"Ok, but some clan is going to have a vomiting skull, and I'm going to be pointing to it and raising an eyebrow."

"Not going to worry…"

Gracie looked around as everyone kept talking. Finally, putting up a hand, she interrupted, "I mean it, guys. Keep being smart-alecky, and you'll wind up with something olive green, which doesn't go with anything in anyone's wardrobe *ever*."

"Oooh, camo," Alan cooed. His character twirled, her blonde hair flying out around her head. "That would…*look terrible with these robes*."

"I will dress you all in olive green burlap sacks," Gracie threatened.

"That would probably suit me, actually," Chowder chimed in. "Especially if I could put it over my head."

"With no pants, that would be a particularly interesting look," Lakhesis muttered.

Everyone burst out laughing.

"As someone whose head is around groin level," Kevin looked up at Gracie, a pleading emote on his character's face, "please don't do that."

"*Guys*," Gracie said a bit desperately, laughing despite herself. "The tabard! Honest to God. *Someone* weigh in on the damned color!"

Alan sighed, taking pity on her. "Red, obviously. No one's come up with a better name than Red Squadron, so we should go with that."

Gracie moved the slider over to the reds and had people weigh in until she selected a faded shade, something that reminded her of the scrappy, battered aesthetic of the Resistance.

"What about a V?" Kevin suggested for the sigil. "For Red Five."

"I like that." Gracie selected it in a very pale gray, and everyone stared at it for a few moments.

They all laughed when Chowder's armor reappeared.

"I know you weren't actually staring at *my* naked body, as perfect as it is in real life," the Ocru said, "but it still felt weird to have everyone looking."

"Says the guy who did the whole burlesque show," Gracie replied affectionately. "I live in Vegas, man, and even *I've* never seen some of those moves."

"Hey, I could come to Vegas and be a stripper!" Chowder gave them all a double thumbs-up. "Women like super-skinny guys who can't dance, right?" He looked around. "Right?"

"Who knows?" Kevin shrugged. "Lots of *guys* like skinny, though."

"Gay guys have all the luck," Chowder muttered.

"Well, that's just not accurate," Kevin added.

Gracie shook her head and chuckled as she paid for the tabard, handing glittering gold coins over to a very lifelike shopkeeper. The whole store was everything one would expect of a fantasy world, from the flickering candlelight—that somehow wasn't too dim to see by—to the bolts of cloth hovering magically in midair along one wall.

Everywhere Gracie looked, there were little details to revel in. A mouse ran along one wall, smudges and dents showed on the heavy wooden counter, and music filtered in from the street. Metamorphosis Online was one of the most immersive places she had ever been, a world so realistic that sometimes she almost felt like she could smell the street food and the smoke from the braziers at each corner.

Of course, the whole effect was somewhat spoiled by the fact that the game's creators hated her guts.

But she was trying not to think about that right now.

A moment later, the guild's founding members burst into cheers as they found themselves dressed in the new tabard. Alan's character looked tiny and delicate, her golden hair and flushed skin adorably set off by the red, and Lakhesis spun around twice to admire the way the cloth lay over her plate armor.

"*Love* this," she said in satisfaction.

"All hail Red Squadron," Gracie called, forcing a smile. She *really* wished she hadn't thought about the game developers, but what was done, was done. "So, what should we do, now that we all look so snazzy?"

"Somehow I sense you're not talking about walking around town all dressed up, letting people bask in our glow," Kevin picked a bit of non-existent lint off his tabard, "and I want you to know I think that's a mistake. This thing is nice, and I don't want to get blood all over it."

"You're not a melee fighter," Lakhesis pointed out, "so if you get blood all over you, someone else isn't doing their job."

"*Still.*"

"I know where we could go," a new voice said.

Gracie looked over quickly, emoting a smile, and there was a round of cheers and greetings. "Anders! Good to see you."

Jay's character gave a flourishing bow. "Hello, all. From

the way I suddenly found myself wearing a tabard, I figured I might find you all here."

"You look good," Chowder said. "Not as good as me, of course…"

"Does anyone look as good as you?" Jay asked philosophically. He slung an arm around Chowder's shoulders.

"No one answer that," Chowder ordered, pointing around at all of them. "Anyway, where are you taking us?"

"Oh, nowhere special." Jay made a show of inspecting his clothing for dust, an especially ostentatious gesture given that in-game clothes never got dirty. "Just…the edge of the world."

"Oooooh," the rest of the team said in unison.

Each zone in Metamorphosis Online was bounded in various creative ways so that players could see the "world" stretching away endlessly in all directions, but could only play in a certain area.

Lately, however, there had been rumors flying around that there was a way to get all the way to the edge of one zone and walk out into nothingness. Some people said the game's moderators hung out there, and others said that the step into the void was actually part of the game's lore.

Whatever the reality, there were a lot of videos online of people searching for the edge…and none of them finding it.

Part of Gracie wanted to protest that they shouldn't try to go places they weren't authorized for, but a larger part of her wanted to explore.

Game glitches were always funny, for one thing.

For another, the game developers already hated her

through no fault of her own, so in her considered opinion, they could suck a bag of dicks.

"Let's go," she said, holding one thumb up, the other hand pointing out. "Lead on, Anders."

Jay had his character gesture toward the door and led the gaggle of guildmates out into the street. As he walked, however, he opened a private channel to Gracie.

"Hey, so keep your eyes open when we get out there. Let's just say there's a particular reason I wanted to go to this zone."

"Really?" Gracie's interest spiked.

"Yeah." Jay sounded like he could barely contain his excitement. "Harry mentioned that he'd initially put some stuff out in the void, and he wasn't sure we'd be able to access it the way he'd intended, but we should definitely look. He said if they didn't find the quest, then they probably haven't found this stuff."

"Hmm." In the real world, Gracie wrinkled her nose. Their characters were striding down the street, surrounded by colorful flags and buildings all jumbled together in differing sizes, while NPCs hawked goods and active characters turned to watch this new guild…and the floating golden 1 over Gracie's head.

That 1 indicated that she was now at the top of the global Top 10, the highest-ranked players, and earning a considerable payout each month instead of paying to play. The other 9 players on the list were all members of sponsored guilds, and Gracie's heading on the list had made her a celebrity in-game.

It was the reason Dragon Soul Productions didn't like her very much right now, and all of it was due to the interference of one of the founders, a now-ousted man named Harry.

Harry had built a quest that boosted a certain player's ranking, and Gracie had managed to start the quest before anyone else. What other advantages it conferred, she wasn't sure. No one seemed to know. What they *did* know was that the other guilds and sponsors in the Top 10 didn't want her waltzing in and stealing their spotlight.

She could really care less from a rankings standpoint, Gracie reflected, but now she wanted to stay number 1 out of sheer spite.

Jay led them to the loading tower for the airship, a dizzy open platform covered in luxurious couches and carpets. NPC butlers stood around the edges, holding trays of various beverages and elegant, fantastical snacks, and a magical shield held the wind at bay, glimmering faintly in the corners of Gracie's vision.

As usual, she plunked herself down in the very center of the platform and did her best not to look around. Lakhesis and Alex were at the edge, trying to jump out onto one of the many elegant metal wings. Both of them thought it was hilarious to see the game world rushing by thousands of feet below, but the mere thought made Gracie shudder.

"Hey." Jay sat his character down next to hers. He had brought two crystal flutes of a purple liqueur, and he handed one over.

Gracie held it up to the light. "What do you think this tastes like? I'm picturing lavender, which…isn't really appetizing?" She laughed. "It's so pretty, though."

"Cotton candy," Jay predicted. "With a kick."

"Sounds about right." Gracie had her character take a sip. "Damn, I actually swallowed. It looks so *real.*"

Jay laughed. "So, glad to have some time before we get there. Harry's been asking about you."

Gracie stilled. She took a deep breath and said nothing.

"I haven't told him much," Jay said hastily. "I know it makes you uncomfortable."

"It does," Gracie agreed. "I just wish I knew why."

When Harry had contacted Jay, it had made sense. After all, Jay had once worked for Dragon Soul Productions and had been fired for refusing to help them cut Gracie's character out of the game. Like Harry, he had a grudge, and unlike Harry, he had up-to-date knowledge of the game. Harry had offered his help to Gracie and Jay so that Gracie could get all the way through the hidden quest before the game's current owners could figure out how to stop her.

"I feel like a pawn in someone else's game," she said finally.

Jay drew in a breath to make a retort but held it back. There was a pause, and then he sighed. "Yeah. I get that. I…"

"Maybe it's that it always sounded like he was *such* an asshole," Gracie continued.

Jay burst out laughing. "Uh, yeah. Yeah, he really was. All of his secretaries quit, he made the junior developers cry on the regular—all that jazz. If he hadn't been a brilliant programmer, he wouldn't have kept his job for as long as he did. *Metamorphosis* is what it is because of Harry, in large part. It was his idea; the others just helped. And they helped a lot, but…" He shrugged and looked out at the clouds rushing by. "I guess I just want the window into all of it, you know?"

"I know," Gracie assured him. The airship was descending now, haptics shuddering in what she considered a *far* too realistic depiction of landing. "I get why *you're* interested, Jay. That's not what makes me worry. What I don't like is wondering whether Harry's trying to use us to nuke the game somehow."

"I *have* wondered that," Jay admitted. "And I like to think we'll be able to see something like that coming. More than that, I feel like if that were his goal, he could have come up with better ways to do it. If he was good enough to weave this quest in without them being able to find it, he could easily crash the servers and make the game fail."

"That's true, I guess." Gracie stood up as the airship landed. "Well, we'll just play it by ear."

"Best kind of plan," Jay agreed. He followed Gracie across the deck to look out at the Twilight Sea. "And even if we don't find it, at least this zone is a gorgeous place to spend some time."

He was right. The town of Night's Edge lay on the edge of a sheltered cove, its buildings shrouded in perpetual twilight. The sun was always on the edge of the horizon here, spilling golden light like a pathway across the sea while the sky above faded to purple. An archipelago of islands stretched away to the north, and Jay pointed to them.

"That's where we're headed. All we have to do is fight our way through a few covens of merfolk, and we're good to go."

Gracie laughed and jumped down from the airship, but

her laugh turned into a shriek when it started to ascend again. Even knowing that she wasn't really falling, she felt her heart lurch.

"Son of a *bitch.* Ugh, I hate heights. All right, everyone, come on! Let's go find the edge of the world."

"Sir?" Sam stuck his head around the door of Dan's office. "You wanted to see me?"

"Yes." Dan looked at Dhruv, who was lounging against the wall with his customary surly expression. Not for the first time, Sam reflected on how different the two remaining founders of Dragon Soul Productions were. Dan was mild-mannered and took pains to be polite, while Dhruv was prone to snapping at employees, and never held back on sharing his bad moods.

The thing was, you could always count on Dhruv to play it straight with you, and he was much more inclined to forgive and forget than Dan was. Sam always forgot that, and he told himself again that he really needed to keep it in mind.

Dan settled back in his chair and assessed Sam with a long glance. "I know you and Jay were…close."

"Somewhat," Sam said cautiously. "We had worked together for a while. I wouldn't say we had any particular friendship." He wished he knew where this was going. Was he getting fired?

"You had managed him for a while," Dan said. "You were familiar with his work."

Sam nodded wordlessly. Either a yes or a no could be dangerous right now.

"So you would be able to follow his trail," Dan said, "if we were to set you to follow him? What we're planning to do is leave a backdoor open in the system for him to access it."

Dhruv cleared his throat.

Dan ignored him. "We want you to keep an eye on what he does. We'll be running frequent backups, so we'll be able to reload if he does anything big, but we mostly want to see where he goes."

Sam blinked. "You're… I'm sorry, you hired Jay back—"

"No," Dan said shortly. "We think he may be well placed to figure out the scope of what Harry inserted, however, and we've given him access to the database."

Dhruv shook his head once, and Sam realized that the two founders were at odds over this plan. He opened his mouth to speak, but there was a ding and Dan leaned forward to look at his computer. His face changed, suddenly alert and unsettlingly predatory.

"They're in Night's Edge," he said to Dhruv. To Sam, he gave a brief nod of dismissal.

Sam hesitated, then left. Neither of them was paying the slightest attention to him anymore, and he frowned as he walked out.

What were they up to?

And did he actually want to help them?

CHAPTER TWO

"Hey, Callista," Lakhesis called.

"What's up?" Gracie's character emerged out of the sea next to Jay and waded onto the shore of a tiny island. This was one of the few times when the unreality of the game world came into focus: characters emerging from the sea in full plate mail, their hair not even damp, not tripped up by the waves that swirled around them.

Gracie found Lakhesis amongst the group and tilted her head curiously.

"You always know the lore, right?" Lakhesis asked. "There's gotta be *something* about this place? Unmoving sun and filled with merfolk?"

"There *is* a cool backstory." Gracie put up with a goodly amount of teasing for caring about the lore so much, but because she knew the group was joking, she still liked to wax poetic about the characters and places in the game. "Everyone up for it?"

"Hell, yeah," Freon said. The frost mage was wading out of the water next to Ushanas, the guild's fire mage.

"We all rely on you to talk to the eighty-five NPCs you need to interrogate to get the whole story. No one else does that."

"Excuse you," Dathok said. As the guild's backup healer, the Ocru male wore cloth robes that looked ridiculous on his tall, muscled frame. "I happen to know a thing or two about this zone."

"Oh?" Gracie sounded excited, and Jay smiled. This was one of the things he liked best about her. She wasn't threatened when someone else shared her interests. She looked at it as a chance to learn. "What did you read?"

"Well, you start with the general backstory. You tell these things better." Dathok made his way over the rocks and toward the other shore. "I'll pick up after— Oh, shit."

"Merfolk!" Freon shouted. There was a burst of ice magic ahead, and the cloth-clad members of the group ran back toward them.

"Fys!" Gracie called. She had taken off at the first hiss of the merfolk, and she unsheathed her massive shimmering sword as she ran. "Summon your Ifrit!"

"Way ahead of you!" Kevin called. A flaming demon charged into battle behind the main melee group, swiping at the merfolk with flaming claws. "No, don't step in the water, you stupid thing! Goddammit!"

Jay was chuckling as he reached his first target and slammed his fist into it. The mermaid gave a shriek and started trying to cast a spell, but Jay kicked and punched to interrupt her casting. He gave a snort of laughter.

"What?" Gracie called.

"I just... I'm punching a mermaid! What a day." He roundhouse-kicked her in the head and nodded in satisfaction when she collapsed. "Feels kinda wrong to beat the crap out of spellcasters, though."

"They didn't have to start shit," Kevin called. "You don't see me going around pissing off giants, do you?"

"Everyone's a giant compared to you," Jay told him.

"Shut up, or I'll hex your shins."

They dispatched the merfolk in short order and collected opals and coins from the corpses, along with a wicked-looking dagger that Mirra and Dathok squabbled over good-naturedly.

"So," Gracie said as they swam out toward the next island. "The Twilight Sea. It's been frozen in twilight since the war between the merfolk and the Aosi."

"The *Aosi*?" Jay asked, surprised. He knew that the various non-playing races had fought one another and that the playing races had done the same, but he hadn't realized there had been wars between the playing and non-playing races.

"Yes, after the races were scattered," Gracie said. "The Aosi were created to bring peace, remember? They totally sucked at it, but they still thought they were better than everyone else. So they got to this zone, waltzed in, and told the merfolk they were here to run everything. The merfolk? Well, let's just say they weren't thrilled by that idea."

"The Aosi *did* just want the land," Dathok pointed out. "And the merfolk would have the water."

"It's still fucking rude," Gracie said. "And they *did* say they were going to rule the whole thing."

"I mean, that's true." Dathok gave an elaborate shrug.

"Anyways," Gracie said, mimicking the gesture, "the

whole fucking situation went into meltdown, and before long, there was a *holy* war going on, because that's clearly what the situation needed. The Aosi were blowing up the merfolks' temples, and the merfolk were blowing up their *own* temples for some reason."

"That was the part I heard about!" Dathok said, enthusiastically. "I had a beer with this grizzled old sailor, and—"

"Wait, a real beer?" Jay tried to picture that scene.

"No, an NPC. In-game beer. Actually, I *was* drinking actual beer at the time." Dathok waved his hands. "Anyway, the Aosi told them that they were part of the end-times prophecy in the merfolk legends, so the merfolk needed to listen to them, right? There had been stories that angels would come to Elakara and, I don't know, save everyone or something. The Aosi had the bright idea of claiming they were the angels."

Gracie murmured, "When someone asks if you're a god, *you say yes.*"

"Precisely," Dathok agreed. "Well, the merfolk thought about this, and *apparently* they decided that if the Aosi *were* the angels, the whole thing was probably crap, so they burned it all down, metaphorically speaking. They created a whole different religion, and blew up all the old temples."

"Oh, *shit*," Alex commented. "That's hardcore."

"Hell, yeah. So they're probably not too glad to see an Aosi show up with a big sword," Dathok pointed out.

"Yeah, yeah," Gracie muttered. She strode across the beach and yelled toward the water, "Just FYI, I'm not here for a fight, so leave me alone and I'll return the favor, okay?"

There was no answer.

"That should work," Alex said drily.

"Oh, absolutely," Jay agreed. "It's one of the cheat codes. I should know."

The group snickered.

"So how did it wind up as twilight?" Alan asked.

"Ah, that," Gracie said. "The Aosi cursed the merfolk. They said their days were numbered, and they would live on the edge of night forever, perpetually going into darkness and never again seeing the sunlight filtering through the water."

Even she sounded a bit uncomfortable now, and she paused as they waded once more into the dark waters to head to the next island. None of them spoke as they swam, and it was only when they were clambering onto the sand that she said in a low voice, "I know these things aren't real, but sometimes I can't help but be sad about them anyway."

Jay realized she had said that last part only to him, and he looked at her and nodded. "I know what you mean," he said quietly. "One of our writers once said to me that stories like this are about using lies to tell the truth. No one in the real world has ever cursed someone to eternal twilight, but it's true, in a way."

Gracie nodded.

Up ahead, Alex and Lakhesis were trying to scramble up a hillside, and they were getting nowhere. A long line of jagged rocks stretched in one direction, and in the others, the magical barriers of a merfolk city could be seen.

"This way," Jay said cheerfully. He looped around the beach to where the rocks were and studied them. There was a small ledge…aha. There. He hopped up, remembering the steps from the various videos he had watched. All of them had followed different routes, and all of them had cut off a few steps up.

He'd noticed something different, however—one of Harry's calling cards, as it were. The man had liked to hide doors, and Jay was fairly certain that there was a hidden portal under one of the ledges that people had been trying to get on top of.

He scrambled under the ledge while Gracie waved the others onto the rocks and peered into the darkness in front of him. "Light spell, anyone?"

"Sec," Ushanas called, and a moment later, a ball of fire floated over next to Jay.

Jay looked at the walls around him, which were reflecting the flickering light, and sighed when the fireball went out. He twiddled his thumbs, and a moment later called, "Ushanas? Another fireball?"

"I'd be glad to," Ushanas said, "if you could tell me where to send it."

"What?" Jay looked around. "Oh, fuck!"

He wasn't near the ledge anymore. In fact, it was hard to tell *where* he was, and he suddenly had the dizzying sensation that he might be falling and not even know it. Panic gripped him, and he wondered if this was how Gracie felt on the airships.

"Get hold of yourself," he muttered.

"I beg your pardon?" Ushanas said. There was a grin in his voice. "Just kidding, man. I know you were talking to yourself. How do we get in there?"

"No idea. I wedged myself under the ledge and must have fallen in somehow." He couldn't see anything, and he couldn't tell which way was up, despite feeling his feet on the floor in the real world. It was immensely disconcerting.

A moment later, however, the rest of the group popped into existence around him, and their uniform alignment provided him with a reference for up and down. Jay breathed a sigh of relief.

"There really is nothing here," Gracie said, awed. "I didn't think it would be so disorienting. Kinda freaking me out, and I *definitely* can't look down."

"Here." Alex had reached out into nothingness. "I gotcha."

"Best roommate ever," Gracie managed. Although they were on opposite sides of the group, their hands met and clasped.

Jay looked around in disappointment. "I don't see anything," he said. "I don't know, let's take some screenshots and head back?"

"Sounds good!"

The group posed for screenshots, danced around in the nothingness, and chattered away to each other as Jay paced methodically around the area. He didn't see anything but had a thought. He wondered if anyone had thought to disable his login yet. If not, he could trace where his character had been and use that to isolate the code for this area. If what Harry had hidden was still here, he might be able to find it that way.

He decided that when he logged out, that was the first thing he would check.

"I told you," Dhruv said to Dan. The Indian man raised a single black eyebrow. "What did you really think there would be?"

Dan didn't rise to the bait. "I thought it was worth exploring. And shouldn't you be happy? As I recall, you were worried about them finding something."

"It's risky," Dhruv said simply.

"And when you have a non-risky plan, I will listen to it." Dan returned to watching. "For now, I'm going to see what he does as soon as he logs out."

CHAPTER THREE

"All right, everyone." Gracie's voice came through the Aosi filter, emerging echo-y and epic-sounding. "I am *exhausted.* I'm calling it a night, but you all have fun, okay?"

"Good night," Alan called. "If we go into any other glitchy zones, we'll take screenshots for you."

"That's all I can ask." Gracie laughed and then gave a yawn that the filters turned into a haunting whisper of sound. "Wow, I feel very epic right now. 'As the prophecy has foretold, indeed.' I am going to snarf down some cold lo mein and go to bed."

"Truly, we are blessed to have a leader so inspired by the gods," Ushanas intoned. "All hail."

"All hail," the rest of them repeated solemnly.

Jay snorted, then yawned. "I'm going to go to bed too. Turns out I'm too old to stay up all night anymore."

"I'm going to look like hell if I don't sleep," Kevin weighed in.

"All right, *everyone* go get some sleep," Gracie said. "That's an order from your gods-appointed leader."

There was a sleepy round of goodnights, then people ported back to their home points and logged out with a series of *bloops*.

When the cozy confines of his favorite inn materialized around him, Jay followed suit.

Alone in his apartment, he took off his headset and yawned widely as he removed his VR suit. He hung it carefully on the stand and ambled into the kitchen to stare at the various half-eaten containers of takeout he'd ordered earlier that night.

He knew he should learn how to cook, but, as always, he put that off for another time. He decided, on reflection, that the remains of the burrito were probably the most edible, and gave a pleased nod as he chewed.

Edible.

Mostly.

He wandered around the apartment as he ate. He'd been living here for three years now, and he'd managed to make the place his own, mostly by accident. There was a ridiculously comfortable couch, gifted to him by the set of college students who'd moved out of the apartment at the end of the hall. He had a framed set of Star Wars prints his sister had gotten him, proffered with some good-natured jokes about how he hadn't grown out of his nerdiness. Then there was the coffee table that was perpetually on the edge of falling apart, and a potted palm he'd managed to keep alive since college. He even had curtains and a rug like a real adult.

He didn't think he *was* a real adult, but someone who

walked into his apartment might mistake him for one. He'd settle for that.

When he finished the burrito, he looked toward the bedroom with a sigh. He knew he *should* get some sleep. He was so exhausted at this point that his eyeballs were dry and his head ached. He should take a shower—in a bathroom that had a proper towel rack, no less—and go to bed in a bed with sheets and a real bed frame, because that was what a reasonable adult would do.

He already knew he wasn't going to do that, however. Instead, he was going to spend a few minutes stressing about breaking into the *Metamorphosis Online* databases, and then he was going to actually do it.

Come on, man, he could hear Gracie saying in his head. *If you're going to do it,* do *it. Shit or get off the pot.* Knowing her, she'd probably throw in some choice speculation about just how many deranged sheep his family tree included.

The thought made him give an undignified snort of laughter, and he went over to his desk with a renewed sense of purpose. If he was going to do this, he *should* just do it—and Gracie was a big part of the reason why. From the little bits and pieces Jay had spliced together, every person in the guild was dealing with something in their life that made the game a necessary escape.

Gracie had built a team that allowed each of them to escape without wallowing.

For the guild's sake, Jay didn't want to burn *Metamorphosis Online* to the ground, which might otherwise be his urge. He didn't particularly trust Dan and Dhruv to run the game world, but he didn't want to nuke anything or cause an explosion that would ruin his guildmates' haven.

So, while he didn't particularly trust Harry, he was going to work with him, because figuring this whole mess out was the only way Jay could think of to solve it.

He let muscle memory take over as he logged into the VPN. Part of why he had held off was his fear that an unauthorized login would be flagged somehow in the system. In a well-run company, his access would have been shut off immediately when he was fired.

But he wasn't entirely surprised when his login still worked. He swallowed, blew out a long breath, and shook his head. The IT team was overworked these days, what with managing the constant stream of glitches, forgotten passwords, and bug fixes their player base ran into. Not only that, Dragon Soul Productions still functioned very much like a small company, without any of the set-in-stone processes a larger corporation would have.

Which gave Jay just the opening he needed. He navigated to the databases that housed the players' progress records and brought up his own. He could track where his character had been over the course of his session tonight, and he followed the trail with his eyes narrowed: Howl's Inn, Kithara, Night's Edge…

Zone 8 DUPLICATE DELETE.

Jay's lips quirked. How many records, from NPC names to zone designations, had been botched somewhere and hastily renamed in anticipation of a cleanup sweep that never came? Crunch time was always a crazy scramble to get the product out the door and shipped, and no one had time to clean out files that weren't causing glitches.

Jay couldn't think of a better way to hide something in plain sight. If this had been Harry's plan, it was a good one.

The zone wasn't actually empty. An empty zone would be sterile gray in color, with visible grids. Zone 8 was entirely black. It had been filled with color, which was part of what interested Jay. The black *could* hide something.

And it did. He fumbled his way through adding a light source, searching online and getting through the process with a large amount of swearing. He had watched some of his colleagues do zone design, but he'd never done it himself. All he had was general knowledge about how the database worked.

It was worth it, though. When he finally managed to add light—an incongruous elegant lantern that floated and cast flickering shadows—he could see what Harry had hidden.

"Son of a bitch," he murmured.

The sword, shield, and armor were some of the most beautiful things he'd ever seen. He could not imagine how much better they would look when he was actually in the game. The armor was arrayed on a custom-built stand and it gleamed faintly, jewels winking in the lantern's light. The sword was suspended next to it, its scabbard a work of art inlaid with runes and mythical creatures, and the shield leaned against the armor stand, the faint light picking out a scene of the scattering of the races.

"Holy shit." Jay fumbled for his phone and typed a quick text to Gracie.

Log in RIGHT NOW.

Sam leaned forward, his eyes narrowing.

He hated this—the deception and the double-crossing. Jay had been his employee, yes, but Sam had always felt a kinship with him. Jay's love of the game world was infectious, and he'd always viewed Sam's relative ignorance about MMOs as an opportunity to share his enthusiasm, not as a reason to snub Sam or look down on him.

And now, Sam was going to be reporting Jay's doings to Dhruv and Dan.

What made it worse, in Sam's opinion, was the fact that he couldn't really justify *not* doing so. If Jay just hadn't broken into the game, there would be nothing to report.

However, Jay had, and there was no excuse for it since this wasn't a matter of life and death. It was just Jay breaking the rules, as he'd always done. He and Sam had butted heads on that score more than once, and now here he was, doing it again.

"Gahhhh." Sam rested his head in his hands and clenched his fingers in his hair. "Why did you have to log in, you idiot? You couldn't just let it be?"

He had to tell Dan and Dhruv. He couldn't afford to lose this job, and Jay *had* done something wrong.

But he wasn't particularly happy to be doing it. He decided to go get a donut first. *Then* he'd tell Dan and Dhruv. He set his computer to record the changes that were flickering through the database and ambled off as slowly as he could reasonably walk.

Gracie had just pulled the covers up and snuggled into bed when her phone buzzed.

"You have *got* to be kidding me." She squeezed her eyes shut and ignored the buzz. "Not important," she told herself. "If it were important, they'd call."

Her phone buzzed again, and curiosity got to her. After all, it wasn't like she had anywhere to be in the morning, right? With a sigh and a curse for whoever was disturbing her, she threw the blankets back and stretched one arm out to feel around on her nightstand.

She ended up knocking her phone to the floor, which resulted in more cursing and some unsuccessful fumbling. Defeated, she turned on the light and squinted her way through finding the damned thing, which had wound up wedged between the nightstand and the bed.

"This had better fucking be good," she muttered. When she saw the text, she groaned. "Noooo," she typed back. "Sleep. Exhausted."

RIGHT NOW, came the return text, insistent. **Equip the stuff I'm putting in your inventory**. A moment later, as if he could sense her internal debate, he sent, **RIGHT NOW. SERIOUSLY.**

"Ughhhhh." Gracie shoved herself out of bed and stumbled out into the main room, rubbing her eyes. She raised an eyebrow blearily at Alex, who was on the couch having a low-voiced phone conversation. He frowned back in a wordless question, and she threw her hands up and shrugged.

"One sec," she heard him say as she started putting on the VR suit. "Uh…Gracie? Whatcha doin'?"

"I don't fucking know." Gracie groaned. "Jay's going on

about some shit. I just want to *sleep*." She put on the head-set, then realized the system wasn't turned on and gave a little moan of frustration. "Augh." She stumbled over and pressed the power button, swaying silently on her feet as it booted up. It seemed to take forever.

"Not entirely sure," Alex said in response to a question Gracie could barely hear. "Um, let me go into another room. I—oh. Okay. Well, I'll see you then." His voice was warm and self-satisfied, which made Gracie grin.

She looked over her shoulder as the game started to boot up. "Was that Sydney?" She had taken it upon herself to slip Alex's number to a waitress who'd been checking him out, and despite Alex's insistence that he never wanted to have another relationship in his life, he'd clearly been enjoying his conversations and dates with her.

"I'm not going to answer that," Alex said loftily. "Weren't you supposed to be asleep?"

Gracie gave him an amused grin. "Did I interrupt something?"

"You might have if it had been a few minutes later." Alex raised an eyebrow. "But it turns out that having a half-asleep zombie roommate in the room doesn't exactly set the mood."

"Whoops," Gracie replied. She dropped the headset onto her head. "Sorry."

"Eh, I should sleep anyway. What are you doing? I'm logging in, wait for me!" He got into his VR suit as well.

"Not sure." Gracie watched the game boot up around her and tilted the headset up so one ear was free. "Jay said to log in and equip... What is *that*?"

"New armor," Alex said after he was in-game. "Whoa, damn, Gracie! Look at those *stats*."

"Those stats," Gracie agreed. "Damn. Where'd he find this?"

"There's a sword and a shield, too," Jay said in Gracie's ear, making her jump.

"Jesus! Goddammit, I didn't know you were online."

"Uh-huh." He was laughing. "Equip it right now, Gracie."

"Okay, okay, okay. What's the rush?"

"I just want to make sure. Well, is it bound to your character now?"

"I…looks like?" Gracie shrugged. "Yeah, it is. Holy *shit*, man, look at my stats now! Where did you *find* this?"

"In that glitch zone we went into," Jay said, sounding self-satisfied. "Seems like Harry's playing straight with us."

"Hmmm." Gracie pondered that, then yawned. Alex yawned too, and quietly logged out.

"Go back to sleep," Jay said. "I just wanted to get this into your inventory since they can't seem to fuck with your account anymore. Get some sleep. We'll talk tomorrow."

"Uh-huh." Gracie rubbed her eyes, shut down the system, and headed back to bed with a series of increasingly loud yawns. Through the partially open bathroom door, she caught a glimpse of Alex turning his head to study his face in the mirror, clearly posing to find his best angles, and she snickered quietly.

Alex could complain all he wanted, but he was clearly head over heels for this woman.

She crawled back into bed and was asleep before she even managed to get the covers pulled up.

"*What* armor?" Dan asked in frustration a few minutes later.

"A set of armor," Sam said through a mouthful of donut. He swallowed hastily when Dan gave him an annoyed look. "Sorry. I stayed late because he logged in, and it's been a long shift. There's the lantern, right?"

"No lantern," Dan said.

"Well, add one. Something for a light source." Sam came to stand next to Dan as the other man navigated through the tables and added a sun in the distance. The zone lit up…

To show an empty armor stand, and no armor, sword, or shield. There was a pause, then Dan looked slowly at Sam.

"You said not to interfere!" Sam pulled the excuse out of his ass.

Luckily, Dan was still a reasonable person. The founder gave a sigh and dropped his head into his hands.

"You're right, I did. You came to get me when he started looking, too. It was out of our hands." He looked up at the screen and shook his head. "But Dhruv is gonna lose his shit."

CHAPTER FOUR

Gracie took a long sip of her smoothie, glanced at the Ralph Lauren store, and sighed. She supposed she should get this over with, but she wasn't looking forward to it.

She needed new clothes desperately. The tank tops and jeans she owned were all falling apart, and she had a ragged assortment of tee-shirts from college 5ks and charity events, but apart from that, there were only the dresses her parents had made her get for family events and the work uniform she had tossed immediately after she quit.

Now that she actually had money coming in every week from *Metamorphosis Online*, she was easily going to be able to make rent, and she had some left over to get new clothing. *Something nice, dear,* her mother's voice said in her head. *Nice, neat clothing. You should always present yourself to your best advantage.*

Why, exactly, she should bother to do that when her "job" was playing a video game, Gracie didn't know, but her clothes were literally getting holes in them. She needed something new. She drained the last of her smoothie, threw the cup in the trash, and sighed as she ambled into the store.

She made her way through the racks with weary resignation. Button down shirts, polo dresses, and khakis lined the racks in neat rows, with billboards of models relaxing on sunny beaches with cable-knit sweaters draped over their shoulders. Everyone was smiling blissfully.

Gracie looked out at the mall and stopped, considering. One of the outlet stores was there, its racks filled with discount cuts that were out of style and definitely *not* classic or preppy looks.

A smile grew on her face as she marched over to the other store and started grabbing things off the racks. Boyfriend-style jeans with rips in them, plain tee-shirts and tanks in colors she liked, and pajama pants with unicorns and rainbows on them. Gracie looked around, smiling, then grabbed a pair of comfy slippers off a nearby shelf as well before heading up to the registers.

She might have money now, but she really didn't want to spend it on clothes she didn't even like. What was the point, anyway? She was going to be relaxing at home, and she had really never bought clothes she liked before. She snatched a dark blue hoodie off a rack nearby and added it to the pile.

If her mom was going to make her go to her sister's engagement party over the 4th of July, then Gracie was fully intending to show up wearing whatever the hell she wanted and not apologize for it.

She gulped. That was the idea, anyway, but the thought

still scared her—and she hadn't told her parents that she was playing video games for a living now.

She took the bulging plastic bags from the saleslady with a smile and ambled out into the crush of the mall before heading to the food court and ordering a number of gloriously inauthentic Chinese dishes. She was just finishing when she noticed a man with a beard and very short hair looking at her.

She frowned. Now that she thought of it, she had seen this guy yesterday too. He'd been at the apartment complex. Gracie had assumed he was a new neighbor, but…

She was seeing him here, too. She shook her head. He probably *was* a new neighbor, and coincidences happened every day. She'd taken years of statistics, so she should know better than to get spooked over something like this. When he smiled and gave her a nod, she nodded back, annoyed at herself.

He got up and ambled away after putting his lunch tray at the bussing station.

See, Gracie? Not a stalker.

As she headed back to her car, her phone buzzed, and she checked it before rolling her eyes. It was a message from Matt, her old boss, who was still trying to get her to come back to work at the casino.

Give it up, dude, she typed before sighing and erasing the message. She shouldn't be rude. Matt's boss, Vince, had fired Gracie a few weeks back, and Matt was genuinely trying to make that right.

The thing was that Gracie didn't *want* to go back. She'd clashed with management since the day she'd gotten there, she'd had to deal with rude patrons, and it wasn't like the pay had been great. Besides, if she went back, Matt was going to keep asking her to work as a cocktail waitress, and Gracie had zero desire to wear a sequined dress and get called "sweetheart" by drunk, handsy businessmen.

She was having a hard time explaining this to Matt without sounding rude.

She dropped the bags of clothes in the backseat and headed home, humming along to an absurdly happy, energetic song on the radio before shutting it off in disgust and continuing the drive one-handed, leaning her head on her left hand.

She didn't know why she was so annoyed at life, the universe, and everything lately. Didn't she have it made? Her paying job was playing video games, she'd scored a non-crazy roommate, she had a whole group of cool friends, and she'd managed to extricate herself from the preppy hell her parents wanted her to live in.

So what was the problem? She frowned as she parked, hauled the clothes out of the car, and wandered up to the apartment.

Although it was midday, Alex was home. He was cleaning the kitchen counters when Gracie came in, and when she got to the living room, she saw that he'd bought new lamps and a rug.

"Uh…Alex?"

"Yeah?" He sounded distracted and stressed.

"What's going on, buddy? You're home from work, and decorating the house. Did you quit?" Gracie popped her head into the kitchen, frowning. "Because—OHHHHH."

Alex froze mid-scrub and his shoulders hunched.

"Should I make myself scarce tonight?" Gracie asked wickedly. "Is there a *date*? Are you hoping to bring a certain lady back here?"

"I, uh…" Alex looked flustered. He tried to avoid her eyes by continuing to clean but wound up dumping orange juice all over the floor as he tried to put a cup in the dishwasher.

Gracie stared at the orange juice for a moment. She was trying desperately not to laugh.

"Let me help you," she finally said as diplomatically as she could. "Why don't you go focus on your bedroom, and I'll clean up out here?"

"Thanks," Alex said gratefully, and he whisked away as Gracie shook her head and carried the new clothes to the washer. She grabbed the kitchen towel before starting it, and as an afterthought, added the towels from the bathroom. She reminded herself to tell Alex to wash his sheets. It had been a while since he'd even entertained the idea of dating, and Gracie didn't want to think about what his room looked like.

Not that she was one to judge. All of her pictures were still leaning against the walls, and her laundry basket was surrounded by a pile of clothing she'd thrown with very bad aim.

Her computer blooped as she headed back to the kitchen, and she looked at it to see a video call from Jay. Smiling, she accepted the call and waved.

"I hope you don't mind me cleaning while we talk," she greeted him. "I'd put it off, you know, indefinitely, but Alex has a date tonight, and he's stressing about the apartment. Look." She picked up the laptop and swiveled it around. "He's gotten new decor and everything."

"Impressive." Jay sounded amused. "Although it sort of makes me feel like I don't have my shit together."

"Ugh. I feel ya." Gracie swiveled the computer back around and shook her head. "On the other hand, this *is* a last-minute mad scramble, so it's not like he does either."

"*I HEARD THAT,*" Alex yelled from the bedroom.

"Less talking, more cleaning," Gracie called back. "*And wash your sheets.*"

Jay started laughing. "So, does that mean you'll have to be holed up in your room tonight?"

"Uh, probably. I hadn't thought of that." Gracie scratched her head and grabbed paper towels to start cleaning up the orange juice. "Having your roommate fighting fake monsters in a VR suit probably doesn't set the mood too well, does it? Argh. I wanted to see what was going on with that armor, too."

"Well, if you log in after this, we should still have time, right?" Jay pointed out. "I want to see about it too. The weird thing is, I told Harry we found it, and I haven't heard anything from him since then."

Gracie said nothing. Her skepticism about Harry still hadn't ebbed, but she didn't want to ruin Jay's fun.

"What if…" She scrubbed the floor and bit her lip, then forced a smile as she peeked back at the computer. "We just decided to bum around and have fun in-game until we heard back from him?"

"Now *there's* a good idea." Jay sounded impressed. "Just not tonight, huh?"

"Yeah. I suppose I should do something other than play games, anyway."

"That sounds like your mother talking," Alex commented as he came into the kitchen to rummage under the sink. "I need a trash bag. Is this where they are?"

"Yep." Gracie looked at him. "And you're probably right about my mother, but I'm also trying not to cock-block you by being in the living room when you get back here with Sydney."

"Oh." Alex looked at her, his face faintly queasy. "I'm honestly not sure if I'll have the balls to ask her to come back."

"Don't be ridiculous," Gracie told him, rolling her eyes. "Don't tell me I might be doing all this cleaning for nothing."

"Right." Alex hastened away again with a few trash bags and Gracie chuckled.

"I think he's right, honestly," Jay said. "There's nothing wrong with spending time in a game, *but...* Maybe you should take a night off. You've been doing pretty much nothing except coordinating game stuff for everyone else. You could, uh, go get a drink or something." There was a pause. "With a friend," he added awkwardly.

"Don't *you* get on my case about not having a boyfriend, too." Gracie's tone was strained. Of all the people in her life, she wasn't keen on Jay telling her to get out there and try her hand at dating.

She was trying not to think about why that was.

"I wasn't," he said quietly. "I just meant, ah... Well, maybe a ladies night or something?"

Gracie was startled into a snort of laughter. "What have

I ever done to make you think I'd enjoy a night of Cosmos and dresses and bitching with my girlfriends?"

"*Now* who's throwing around stereotypes?" Jay asked her. Not too long ago, she'd given him a fiery speech about assuming her character was based on her looks, and she had the sneaking suspicion he wasn't going to let her forget it. "Go bowling and get nachos or something. I'm just saying, have some not-game fun with your friends."

"I don't *have* any friends out here," Gracie said with a sigh.

"Really?" Jay sounded skeptical.

"Dude, why do you think I was playing *Metamorphosis Online* in the first place?" Gracie scrubbed at a coffee stain on the floor.

"Okay, you make a good point." She heard him take a drink of something. "Well, a night off, anyway. I'll bum around in-game and—"

"Nuh-uh." Gracie stood up and leaned on the counter, mock-glaring at him. "If I have to take a night off, so do you, Mr. Poking-Around-in-the-Databases."

Jay grumbled but nodded. "All right, and I'll stop distracting you while you clean. Tell Alex to have a good date."

"Will do." Gracie waved and ended the call, going back to scrubbing the counters with a sigh.

Going out for bowling and nachos didn't sound half bad, really. The problem was that Alex was the only person she knew here that she could have done that with, and he was going to be out on a date with an awesome person.

Which she wasn't upset about. She'd helped set it up, after

all. It was just that it was more clear than she wanted it to be that she still didn't have any friends in this city, and she didn't have a date for the evening—or even the prospect of one.

The washing machine dinged, and Gracie went to change over the clothes. She scowled when she saw the slouchy jeans and big sweatshirt. A few hours ago, she'd been so amused to be getting clothes she'd be comfortable in. She'd been laughing at the thought of her mother being scandalized by how unappealing her clothes were.

The fact was, she didn't have anyone to impress.

Gracie sighed as she started the dryer. She wanted to call Jay back to explain why she'd gotten so prickly about the dating comment, but no matter how much her heart leapt sideways when she thought about that, she still didn't have close to enough courage to do it.

She shook her head to clear it and headed into the living room to do a last sweep for takeout containers.

It might not be fun to hide miserably in her room while Alex had a date, but it was a hell of a lot less scary than being honest with Jay.

"Because it's not just information-gathering anymore!" Dhruv slammed his hands on the desk and leaned in, his teeth clenched. "You are *actively helping her.*"

"I am getting information," Dan argued. He rubbed a hand across his forehead and sighed. "If we didn't have a line through to them—"

"No." Dhruv stabbed a finger at him. "*No.* Because they

never would have thought to go to that zone if you hadn't suggested it!"

Dan said nothing. Dhruv was right, and he knew it. Dan had fumbled this. If he were just more patient, he would have told Jay to go hunting, and then sat back and said nothing more. But he'd wanted to go farther and faster, so he'd begun prompting the other man, feeding him clues and letting him in on his personal suspicions.

Dan waited. The tirade was coming. When Dhruv got angry, he yelled. Those last few weeks before they got Harry out had been a storm of shouting so constant that Dan was surprised either man had a voice left. Things had quieted down since Harry left, and Dan didn't want it all to start again.

He'd also admired Harry, in some ways. The man had always stood for *something*, even when that particular something was idiotic or patently insane. Dan, meanwhile, had only stood for being the peacemaker, the bridge between Harry and Dhruv, or Harry and a contractor, or Dhruv and whoever he was angry at that week.

When Harry had gone off the deep end, Dan had chosen to back Dhruv since he was the more functional of the two, better able to get the game off the ground and bring it to fruition. Harry might say he had come up with the idea of *Metamorphosis Online*, and that was true, but the other truth was that he'd never have gotten anywhere if Dan and Dhruv hadn't been on board. They'd spent years helping Harry get out of his own way and smoothing ruffled feathers when he insulted vital employees or failed to come through on his own deliverables.

The idea had been his, but the blood, sweat, and tears had been largely Dan's and Dhruv's.

To Dan's surprise, Dhruv didn't yell this time. He dropped into the other chair and stared Dan down, propping his feet on the desk. He knew Dan hated that, but right now it didn't seem to be an effort to piss Dan off. Dhruv was just thinking.

"Since when are you the impatient one?" Dhruv asked finally.

Dan shrugged, but he felt a smile tug at his mouth. "Wish I knew. Harry being back in the mix…worries me. I just wanted it done with."

Dhruv nodded. "You never did like a fight."

"Who does?" Dan asked acidly. A moment later, he frowned. "Did you two actually *like* squabbling like that?"

Dhruv shrugged noncommittally, although his smile suggested the answer was yes. "Gives me a chance to get all the anger out, no?"

"Oh, for fuck's sake." Dan sank his face into his hands. "We do not have *time* for that. We never have time for that."

"Even less time now," Dhruv reminded him. "So stop moaning and get some coffee. We need a new plan. This one isn't working."

CHAPTER FIVE

The most disorienting thing about the *Metamorphosis* world, Gracie decided, was that they hadn't figured out how to make it have smells. She was walking around Kithara now, listening to the calls of the vendors and the music filtering out of the taverns, and while she could hear the sizzle of cooking food or see signs for bakeries, she couldn't *smell* any of it.

Then again, it was probably best not to smell anything in a medieval city. She wrinkled her nose.

A whistle filtered through the air and she rolled her eyes.

"That's, what, the tenth person to whistle at you?" Kevin asked from somewhere near her knees. The Piskie summoner strode along at Gracie's side, the amarok slinking behind her.

"Probably." Gracie shrugged. "And you should try riding the amarok. If you stood on its back, you'd be...well, almost sternum-high, anyway."

"I tried. It didn't work." Kevin's character waved her

hands moodily. "But probably better than if I'd tried to ride an actual wolf."

"Let's test that! Can you think of anyone you don't like?" Gracie grinned until she heard another whistle, then sighed. "Or we could just use one of those yahoos."

"Well, you know what they say," Kevin replied. "It's not politically correct, but if you don't want to get noticed, you shouldn't wear a giant suit of bright gold plate mail covered in jewels."

Gracie choked on a laugh. "Okay, fair." The suit of armor Jay had found for her was eye-catching in the extreme, and she knew that the players passing her probably wondered where she'd gotten it.

That, or they had noticed the hovering 1 over her head, showing that she was the global Top 10 player. Her team's month-first run-through of the latest content had been what Jay had succinctly described as a "Big Fucking Deal" on the forums. Gracie had avoided them, not wanting to see what people were saying, but the rest of the team seemed to be enjoying their celebrity status.

It was unfortunate, Gracie thought, that she couldn't go incognito in terms of her ranking. It was also unfortunate that this particular suit of armor was the most eye-catching thing she'd ever seen in-game.

"The shield probably doesn't help," she said glumly.

"Nor does the fact that your sword clashes horribly with the rest of it," Kevin added with a sniff. "What are you going to do about that? I twitch every time I look at it."

"Welllllll." Gracie drew the word out. "I could put an illusion on it, I guess. Or I could enjoy the fact that it makes you tweak out."

"Noooo. You're *mean.*"

They had reached the heart of the city, and Kevin led the way into a shadowed temple and up a flight of curving stairs. On the second floor of the temple, a walkway hugged the edges of the building. Trailing flowers only partially obscured the view of the altar below, and around the walls were portals to different zones.

"Where are we going?" Gracie asked Kevin.

"I wanted to explore Night's Edge a bit more," Kevin explained. "I don't know why. It just… It feels like there's more there than what we saw last time."

"That place spooks me," Gracie said with a shudder. "But sure, let's go."

"You're a good sport. Thanks." Kevin took off running and leapt through the portal to Night's Edge with a high-pitched squeal. "Whoooooo!"

Gracie stifled a laugh with one gauntleted hand and followed. The world melted away around her, and there was a moment of rippling ether before reality returned and she was in Night's Edge, with lanterns gleaming in the half-darkness.

Kevin was waiting nearby, his amarok's blue-white fur glittering in the lantern light, and he looked around in interest. "Which way do you want to go?"

"You didn't have a plan?"

"Not specifically. Just wander through town, talk to the NPCs, look around the zone…" The Piskie gave an elaborate shrug. "You know one of the worst things about this game? You get used to emoting a lot with gestures. People at work think I'm nuts now."

"See, this is why you do what I do," Gracie joked. "Piss

off an asshole, get fired, and then start making money from video games. You never have to leave your apartment, and you just get to sit in your pajamas all day. It's great."

Not entirely great, of course, but she didn't want to bum Kevin out. She started along one of the side streets, looking around curiously at the buildings. Everything here had a strange feel to it. The Aosi buildings, even the rough ones, had an otherworldly elegance to them, but those had long since fallen into disrepair and been added onto by humans and even merpeople. Rough construction and shell decor coexisted with dingy, elegantly-sculpted stone edifices.

"Oh, that's right. You're living the high life." Kevin sounded envious. "And you live with Alex, right? But you're not together."

Gracie snorted at the idea. "Noooope. In fact, he's out on a date right now. Third night in a row."

"With the same person?" Kevin sounded bemused.

"Do you really never have relationships?" Gracie asked curiously. "Getting to know so many people, and investing so much time and energy in each one... It just sounds exhausting."

"I don't know. I have a low tolerance for bullshit." The Piskie shrugged. "I start talking to someone, and it's not long before they say something stupid, and I'm out."

"Do you ever maybe think that you're writing people off too quickly?" Gracie raised an eyebrow in the real world, knowing it wouldn't translate into the game. "Hey, this looks cool. Let's go down here."

"Down the creepy, poorly lit alley?"

"It's a video game," Gracie said, amused. "I don't get to do stuff like this in real life."

"Eh, I suppose. Let's send the amarok in first, though." Kevin's character made a complicated gesture and the amarok slunk into the shadows.

Kevin and Gracie trailed behind, Gracie's fingers fairly itching with the urge to draw her sword. Kevin was right, this alley reeked of being a place you didn't want to go at night. She couldn't stop grinning, though. She got to do stupid things in this world and not worry. It was awesome.

"Hey, guys," said Jay's voice.

Gracie jumped and swore, and she heard Kevin's squeaky Piskie voice say, "*Son of a bitch.*"

"Uh." Jay sounded a bit confused.

"Woof." Gracie bent over slightly, her hand over her heart. "Holy crap. That scared the shit out of me."

"Er." Jay waited a moment. "Can I ask why?"

"We're in a dark alley," Kevin explained. "Gracie had this bright idea to go wandering into danger in Night's Edge, and— *OH SHIT, IT'S A SPIDER! IT'S A GIANT FUCKING SPIDER!*"

"*Jesus Christ.*" Gracie drew her sword and shield by instinct, only to give a shriek as the spider came skittering out of the darkness. "Holy shit! Oh God, oh God, oh God, fuck me sideways. I hate spiders!" She raised the shield as the spider's fangs plunged toward her and stabbed up with all her might.

There was a scream and a gush of glowing blue blood, then silence.

Gracie stood frozen, trying not to breathe. "It's all over me, isn't it?" She turned around to see Kevin with his character's hands clapped over her mouth. Blue blood was sliding down the golden plate mail and dripping onto the ground.

Laughter caught her ears, and she wrenched off her headset to look at Alex.

"What the fuck just happened?" Alex was looking excessively well-groomed in a tight-fitting t-shirt and dark jeans. He gave Gracie a rakish grin when she noticed the lipstick on his neck. "It's been a better night on my end, I think. No giant spiders."

"Just you wait," Gracie said darkly and plunked the headset back on. "Okay, I admit my mistakes. Let's GTFO."

"Way ahead of you," Kevin called from the mouth of the alley.

"You left me here alone with a giant spider corpse?"

"I'll do a lot for my friends, but not that." Kevin made no apologies as Gracie came back out into the street. "Oh good, the armor is clean again. Let's try to forget this ever happened."

"Right. Hi, Jay. Want to join us?"

"I'm not sure I do." Jay sounded like he was laughing. "Just kidding, I'm on my way. Had a weird discussion with Harry, by the way."

"Who's Harry?" Kevin asked.

There was a pause. "Former coworker," Jay said smoothly. "You know that I worked at Dragon Soul? Anyway, he's worried the quest line Gracie's on might have been deleted."

"That wouldn't be the worst thing," Gracie pointed out. "Then maybe the devs would leave me alone."

"There's a purpose to it," Jay argued, "and I want to

know what it is. For now, though, let's see what Night's Edge has that *isn't* creepy alleys."

"Agreed," Alex said. "Although watching Gracie fight one from the other side of the VR headset was *hilarious.*"

"I will kill you 'til you die from it," Gracie told him. "And then sic the giant spiders on your corpse."

CHAPTER SIX

Kevin and Gracie were firmly ensconced in a well-lit tavern by the time Jay arrived. Although the game had long-since restored their gear to being perfectly clean, both of them kept looking at their hands and bodies as if to make sure that they weren't still dripping glowing blue spider blood.

"So, where should we go next?" Jay asked. He sat down at the table, his character carrying a large mug of beer. "An all-alley tour of Night's Edge?"

Gracie gave a full-body shudder. "Have fun. May your death be everything you hope for."

"We'll mourn you from here," Kevin chimed in. "Gimme that beer."

Jay laughed as the door opened and Alex came in. There had been plenty of opportunities to upgrade his pet into something rarer, but he had stuck with Teef, the panther he'd gotten at level 2. He also went to go buy a pixelated drink, then came to sit, Teef lurking at his side.

"Good date?" Gracie asked.

Alex said nothing for a moment, then looked up to see everyone staring at him. "Oh, right—facial expressions don't translate. Yeah. Yeah." He couldn't quite keep the grin out of his voice. "*Real* good date."

"*Ha*," Gracie said.

"I don't know what *you* have to be triumphant about," Alex said smoothly. "Because you had nothing to do with her getting my number in the first place, right? You *swore*."

Gracie froze and had her character take a sip from her beer. "I mean, uh—"

"Uh-huh." Alex shook his head. "Well, whatever. You're absolved. Pity you can't seem to pick as well when it comes to guys."

Jay shifted uncomfortably. His feet were aching, he told himself. They should make the most of their playtime. Or something.

Anything to avoid this topic.

"Should we go adventuring?" he asked lightly. "Kevin, you said you thought there might be other things in this zone?"

"Yeah." Kevin sounded meditative. "It has a different feel than some of the others, don't you think?"

"I suppose." Jay considered the topic. If Harry had suggested he look here, and the gear had been hidden here… "I wonder when this zone was created?" he said half to himself. "I wonder if it was one of the earliest ones."

Gracie looked at him with a wordless question.

"When Harry was still on the project," Jay explained.

"What's going on?" Alex asked.

"Something about an old coworker of Jay's," Kevin explained. His character, visible only because she was standing on her chair, shrugged her tiny shoulders. "I don't know, I guess it's possible. He didn't say?"

Jay shook his head and drained his beer, appreciating the play of colors in the mug. "No. He's being really cagey about it."

"Because he's up to something," Gracie cut in. Her voice was quiet but authoritative. "Every time you tell me about him, Jay, something feels *off*."

Jay swallowed. There were a hundred things he wanted to say, but he knew she wouldn't respond well to any of them. She wouldn't approve of him doing this for *her* sake, both because it was trouble he was going to on her behalf and because he'd learned that Gracie *hated* anything that felt like pity or a handout.

He guessed it was part of why she disliked her ranking so much. Although her grasp of the game had let her go toe to toe with some of the top guilds, and she had started this by beginning a quest anyone could have begun and then fighting tooth and nail to triumph, Gracie didn't like the randomness of it all.

Once she had admitted to Jay that it was a knife's edge. "What if I hadn't decided to help the kobolds? What if I'd been tired that night, or had decided to ask a different NPC about the lore?"

Jay hadn't had an answer that satisfied her—not then, at least. But everything in him told him that it *hadn't* been random...not exactly. Gracie had come through this so far because of what and who she was. If she had washed out on any of those quest fights, who was to say what would have happened? She had triumphed, however, because she thought quickly and led her team well.

"Jay?" Alex's voice was tentative.

He'd been quiet for far too long, and Gracie was looking away.

"Sorry, I was thinking about what Gracie said." Jay cleared his throat. "The thing I keep coming back to is that I want to figure out what's going on. This is just one of the ways I'm trying."

Gracie said nothing for a moment, but then she nodded. "Yeah, I get that. Let's go, then."

"I just want to be clear," Kevin said, hopping down from his chair, "that I was just talking about poking around and *seeing* if we find anything. There's a very grim 'you can't handle the truth' vibe going on right now, and that was *so* not what I was going for today."

Gracie gave a snort of laughter. "Right. It's just kind of a bummer that ever since I've gotten here, things have been weird, you know? I'd just like to enjoy the freaking game."

"Minus the spiders?" Alex asked wickedly.

"Mention spiders again and you're going to wake up with some in your bed," Gracie said darkly. "I'll do it, too. See if I don't."

Alex was still laughing as Kevin—knee-high to most of them, even with his elaborate hairdo—led the way through the shadowed streets.

"Let's start at the water," Gracie suggested suddenly. When everyone looked at her, she shrugged. "The Aosi claimed this from the merpeople, right? That makes the shore the clash of worlds, so to speak. I bet there's some cool stuff there, lore-wise."

"Solid." Kevin nodded in agreement and pointed with

both hands. "That way, then. Easy to tell, since everything slopes down to the water."

They followed him, conversation lapsing as they took in the sights and sounds of Night's Edge. Last time they had been overwhelmed by the newness of it and excited about their trip out to the glitchy area, but this time they were here to appreciate what was around them.

There was a haunting melody playing. Like most games, *Metamorphosis Online* had a background soundtrack, but the ambient music wasn't usually so definitive. Night's Edge was supposed to be a town ever poised on the *brink* of night and death, but the melody, which seemed to come from everywhere, spoke clearly of things that had already been lost and would never be recovered. The music spurred Jay ahead, wanting to seek comfort and give it—

He remembered at the last minute that there was no way to take Gracie's hand in this world, so he dropped his back to his side and fell back before she noticed him.

As they approached the water, the bay stretching out before them, the stately Aosi buildings trailed away and were replaced by shanties, some human and some obviously built by the merpeople. Channels of water had been cut down to the sea, and wide pools glimmered in the darkness of the huts.

There was a bad feel to the place, now that they were paying attention. Jay could see everyone scanning restlessly ahead, waiting for the attack.

It wasn't long before it came: a group of three, two humans and a merman, their faces shadowed.

"Adventurers," one of them growled. "They think

because they fight for their lords, they'll be safe here. But this isn't a battlefield with pretty posturing."

"Behind us." Gracie's voice was sure. "They're going to surround us. What do you think, guys? Want the fight?"

"Always," Jay said before he thought. When the rest looked at him, he shrugged. "What? It's been a hard few weeks."

Kevin laughed and made a ball of fire dance in the Piskie's palm. "I'm up for it too.

"Good," Gracie replied, 'because there are *definitely* more behind us."

"On it." Jay pivoted smoothly and gave a shallow bow to the three mermen coming up behind him. "Shall we?"

Behind him, he heard Gracie charge toward the other group with a battle cry, and Kevin's amarok charged into the fray with him. There was the twang of bowstrings and Alex's encouraging shouts.

Definitely one of Jay's favorite things about the group was that Alex tended to try to encourage everyone, and he was incredibly wholesome about it. It was both hilarious and jarring to have someone tell you very earnestly that they *totally* believed in your ability to beat someone to death with a staff.

The first merman rushed at Jay, knocking his character onto his back. The world went blurry with the knockback debuff, and Jay could make out the blue-white blur of the amarok defending him. He bounced on his feet and tapped his fingers while he waited for his character to get up. It was only a two-second debuff, but it felt like years.

He launched into motion as soon as he was back in the

fight. He had more hit points than the amarok, so he made it a point to gain threat on each of the three mermen.

"Take that!" he called, punching the first one in the face. "And that," he added to the second, jabbing an elbow sideways. "And *that*," he finished, kicking the last one in his vaguely-defined groin. "If you've got anything there. Nope, doesn't look like you do." A second kick to the chest sent the merman sliding back. "That's better."

"Everyone okay over there?" Gracie called.

"We're doing all right," Kevin called back. "Want any DOTs on yours?"

"Always. More DOTs, more DOTs, more DOTs. Okay, you can stop with the DOTs, goddamn it."

Laughter, his and theirs, reverberated as Jay worked to kill the first of his targets. The merman was almost as tall as Jay right now—meaning that he was much taller if his tail was extended—and he was *jacked*. It was easy to forget that Jay's character was covered in muscle and feel as if maybe he'd made a terrible mistake.

But there was nothing for it except to fight. Jay swung, stringing combinations together and tapping his fingers in complicated motions to activate buffs and abilities. There was a strange peace in this, he thought. He couldn't think too far ahead, and he couldn't get lost in his thoughts. He just had to keep going.

Gracie and Alex were still working on their three when Kevin and Jay finished up, and Jay popped a health potion before heading in to help with cleanup. It wasn't long before the gang was alone again, gold glittering in their pockets.

"That was more exciting than usual without Alan here

to heal us," Gracie said. She laughed a little. "Oof. This place really doesn't want to be explored, does it?"

"Not so much," Kevin agreed. "And I should be up early tomorrow, so I may head out."

"Likewise," Alex chimed in. "I've got a new client coming in tomorrow. Software dude. 'Alex, you're a nerd. You work with him.'" He imitated his boss's voice with clear annoyance. "Night, all."

"G'night," Gracie said. She looked at Jay. "Welp, don't think we should try this as a party of two."

"Another drink?" Jay suggested. "Or a stroll through the more well-lit places in the city, maybe?"

"Ha-ha. I will take you up on that stroll." She sheathed her sword and headed back up the hill with him. "I don't know what Kevin thinks is here. There are a couple of quests, and it's cool to look at, but it mostly seems like a set piece, you know?"

Jay took his time answering. "What you said," he replied finally. "About how this zone doesn't *want* to be explored? I think you're right."

"Oh?" Gracie looked at him. He wished he could see her face since her character had the same flat, distant expression as usual.

"I think Harry wanted to make this zone look really cool but be somewhere that people wouldn't stick around," Jay said. "I think he wants *us* to stick around, though. Maybe he thought you might because you like righting wrongs. That's how you got the quest in the first place. I think we should keep looking when we have a full group."

"Oh," Gracie said quietly. There was a long pause, broken only by the crunching of her boots on the ground.

"Is everything okay?" Jay asked her.

"Yes, it's… Of course." There was another pause, and he heard her draw a deep breath. "Or maybe not. Am I just a puzzle to you?" Her voice was light, but Jay heard genuine worry there.

Suddenly, he understood. Gracie was afraid that once Jay figured out the quest, he was going to lose interest in the guild.

In her.

He wanted to laugh and tell her how ridiculous that was.

He also wanted to throw up at the idea of telling her how he actually felt, so instead, he let his breath out in a whoosh and shook his head. He was trying to come up with the right words, but between all of the things rocketing around in his head that he *couldn't* say, and the fact that he seemed not to be able to figure out jack shit where Gracie was concerned, he couldn't come up with anything.

Finally, in a stroke of pure luck, he found the right thing: "You're my friend, Gracie. This quest or no, *Metamorphosis* or no, you're my *friend.*"

There was a pause, and then she had her character emote a smile.

"I'm glad," she told him, and there was feeling there.

"I want to solve this," Jay said, "so you can feel like you're just playing the game and experiencing the world. Does that make sense? I want to clear this up so it can stop hanging over us."

"Yeah." She nodded. "Yeah, that does make sense. I get it. By the way, am I the only one leaning into this hill and almost overbalancing?"

Jay snorted with laughter. "No, I'm doing it, too." As they made their way up the winding streets, they found themselves automatically leaning forward the way they would have to in order to keep their balance in real life. His laughter turned into yawns a moment later. "Goddammit, I wanted to stay and talk."

"Get some *sleep*," Gracie said. "We'll come back tomorrow with Alan or Dathok or someone. I think Lakhesis said we got a couple of new healers."

"I wanted to talk to you about that. We're probably going to have moles coming in from the other guilds."

"Jesus Christ!" Gracie exclaimed.

"Sorry I mentioned it. Should have saved it for a better time."

"Nah, it's fine. Just, ughhhh." She drew the word out and sighed. "We'll worry about it tomorrow. Let's turn in, and then sleep late because we're both jobless hobos."

Jay gave a bitter laugh. "I take it you feel as weird about it as I do, huh?"

"A hundred percent," Gracie confirmed. "It fucking sucks. And we can't complain, because we're making a living from playing video games, right?"

"Yeah," Jay commiserated. He sighed. "Maybe we should just accept that someday we'll look back on this as the good old days when we didn't have to wear real pants and *did* make all our bills by playing video games. Sure, maybe we're eating a lot of ramen, but we have a good group here. We could be doing worse."

She smiled at him. "I like that. Good point. All right, sleep. I'll see you tomorrow."

T had woke up to faint light filtering under the door of his room. Frowning, he sat up and felt around in the darkness for a sweatshirt, then stumbled over to the door and opened it.

The light was coming from the common area. The members of Demon Syndicate lived in a renovated warehouse, with one of the upper floors converted into various living areas. Most of the guild members shared rooms, with a big common area, while the guild's officers had a smaller area reserved just for them.

Generally, sleep and exercise rules were pretty well enforced, but Thad knew who was up, and why. A few days ago, Callista's guild had managed a month-first run, beating out Demon Syndicate, and the guild's officers had decided to infiltrate her group.

Jamie had been chosen. As a healer, he had a natural in. He wasn't a tank, which might threaten to displace Callista, and good healers were in short supply. For the past few days, he'd been logging in under a new account, power-leveling a new healer who didn't have any ties to Demon Syndicate, and his schedule had been shifted accordingly.

He looked up as Thad came into the room and gave the leader a quiet nod. Tall and fairly muscular, Jamie looked intimidating to people who didn't know him. If someone met him on the street, there was no way in hell they'd guess what he did for a living, and some of the guys in the guild were a bit salty about it. They were all in pretty good shape now, thanks to the guild's exercise requirements, but Jamie had taken to it better than most.

Thad fought down a wave of resentment. Jamie had the sort of looks that made people listen to him, choose him, notice him. Since Jamie had become the top healer, the leadership at BrightStar, the guild's sponsor, had pushed for him to be included in promo materials and leadership.

Jamie wasn't a leader, though. He hated conflict, he hated making hard decisions, and he didn't like being the center of attention. Thad was fairly sure that Jamie had turned down offers to be the guild leader.

He wanted to hate Jamie for that, but Jamie was too nice.

For instance, right now, Jamie was genuinely sad. He knew that Thad had wanted to infiltrate Callista's guild himself, and he didn't want things to be weird between the two of them.

"How's it going?" Thad asked him bluntly. He went over to the coffee maker and poured himself a cup.

"It's caffeinated," Jamie said worriedly.

"I know." Thad didn't like the attempt to play nursemaid. He took a sip. "How's it going?" he asked again pointedly.

Jamie refrained from sighing. He sat down to his breakfast of oatmeal and a banana and gave a shrug. He paid pointed attention to his food to avoid looking up.

"Fine, I guess," he said.

Thad ground his teeth. He looked back toward his bedroom. Jamie didn't want to talk about this, and neither did Thad. He wasn't going to enjoy hearing about the job he'd wanted to do. But Thad *was* the guild leader. He should know. He sat down at the table.

"Jamie, come on. You got picked. It's fine."

Jamie looked up at him. "It made more sense to have a healer than a tank go over."

Thad took a sip of his coffee and didn't answer.

Jamie waited for Thad to say something more but finally broke. "They're nice," he said awkwardly.

Thad waved his hand for Jamie to keep talking. The coffee was strong, and he was beginning to regret drinking it. Tomorrow would be a struggle.

"I told them I'd played WoW and stuff, but hadn't played this before, so they're treating me like a newbie," Jamie explained. "It covers my ass if I know things about basic formations, so it's a good story. A couple of the guild officers have helped me level."

"Of course they have," Thad muttered. "Gotta show how *nice* they are."

"It's not like that," Jamie argued. "They aren't trying to beat us out or be high up in the rankings. They just want to have fun playing the game, so they'll be like, 'oh, you're at level 18, you should come to this zone. It's really fun.'" He shrugged. "They really like the lore and stuff."

"Well, it's nice to know they're beating us without even

trying," Thad growled savagely. He stood up and grabbed a banana from the bowl on the table. "Guess I'll go read up or something so I can try to keep this guild on track."

He left without another word.

When he was gone and the door was closed, Jamie sighed and let his head drop into his hand for a moment. He hadn't meant to rub in Thad's face that they'd lost the last month-first title.

The healer wasn't at his best right now, though. Red Squadron tended to play really late at night for some reason, so he'd flipped his schedule around to play with them, and he was tired and distracted.

Not only that, trying to avoid problems in conversations with this guild's leader was basically like walking through a minefield. He chewed a mouthful of oatmeal contemplatively. Thad was a quick decision-maker and liked being in charge, which, combined with his natural skill at strategy, made him a good leader. But he was also prone to envying anyone else when they got attention or promotions, or anything at all.

Still, he'd been one of the only people who'd taken the time to teach Jamie how to be a good healer. It had been way back in the day, and Jamie had wound up in a PUG with some members of Demon Syndicate. After the first time they wiped, he'd braced for yelling.

Instead, Thad had asked if he wanted pointers. Over the next few days, they had run almost all the existing dungeons as Thad helped Jamie incorporate new skills and game mechanics, and Jamie had worked his way up through the guild.

Jamie finished his oatmeal and carried the bowl over to

the sink to rinse it out. Thad was willing to be patient and help other people, he reflected, because that meant that Thad was in charge. That he was being benevolent, lifting up someone who was clearly beneath him.

A moment later, he felt bad for thinking that. He finished his coffee and put the mug in the dishwasher, then headed back to the deserted VR gym.

Thad had given Jamie the chance to get into Demon Syndicate, and now Jamie lived rent-free while making as much as he had in his last, much crappier job. He knew that anywhere he went, there would be power dynamics and bosses with annoying quirks. Thad was a good friend most of the time, and Jamie didn't want to lose that.

Which meant there was only one thing to do: figure out what Red Squadron was doing that was boosting them in the rankings so that Thad could use that information to put Demon Syndicate on top again.

Then all of this craziness would die down, and the BrightStar executives would stop trying to make Jamie the next guild leader. Even the thought made him feel vaguely nauseated. It was worse because they never asked outright, they just recommended him for things and gave each other significant looks.

When they were number 1 again, Jamie told himself, this would all stop. Thad would be happy, BrightStar would be happy, and Jamie could go back to having a cool job and a better friendship with his guild leader.

He got himself into his VR suit and logged in. He didn't really like practicing on his own in this big space because the empty room was a bit creepy at night, but the rest of the guild was asleep right now.

"Hey, Cas." The voice that greeted him was Aosi and echo-y—Callista. Jamie had chosen the name 'Caspian,' a reference to one of his favorite characters in the CS Lewis books, and he'd quickly acquired a nickname in the group.

"Hey," Jamie said. His heart had started pounding, as it always did when he talked with Callista.

She was the reason everything was wrong. She was the one he had to deceive, and it made him nervous.

"Get anything tasty?" asked another voice, rumbling and low. That was Dathok, Red Squadron's secondary healer, who had been helping Jamie get up to speed. "He was off getting some breakfast," Dathok explained. "Or maybe lunch?"

"Dinner, lunch, something." Jamie accepted this safe topic with relief. "I have a few weeks free, so I've given up on having a schedule."

"I know how that feels," Callista said. "It gets disorienting, doesn't it?"

"*Yes*," Jamie said emphatically. "It feels kind of...." His voice trailed off. His character walked out of an inn to look at a vista of waterfalls and lush jungle.

"Kind of?" Dathok prompted.

"Eh, I don't want to be insulting. I know it's not really pathetic, it just kind of feels like everyone else is out doing their job and I'm just screwing around, you know?" He missed hanging out with the rest of his guildmates, doing his regular exercise and training routines.

"Are you kidding?" Dathok asked. "I'd kill to have a few weeks free to play *Metamorphosis*. You're doing something right, kid."

"No, he's right," Callista argued. "I've been doing this as

a job, and it feels really weird. I never get out anymore, and I don't see many people. If Alex didn't live here, I'd basically be a hermit. And…well, he has Sydney now, so he's out a lot."

"Alex is Gary Swiftbolt," Dathok explained to Jamie. "He and Callista are roommates."

"You can also call me Gracie," Callista said.

"Nah, I like using people's character names," Jamie said. "It's more fun that way, you know?" In reality, he didn't want to get too close to these people. He knew Thad would practically be taking notes, trying to get into their heads and learn whatever he could to get under their skin, but Jamie just wanted to focus on business.

Using someone's real life against them felt awful.

"Fair enough," Gracie replied easily. If she sensed the lie, she gave no sign of it. "Dathok says he's been helping you level up. You two need a tank?"

"That'd help," Dathok said. "Give Caspian here plenty of time to figure out the ropes without worrying about DPS getting beaten up."

"Solid. Where do you want to meet? Caspian, I see you in Hothik Bay, is that right?"

"Yeah." Jamie swallowed and told himself that it was *good* that Callista was coming to play. She might drop some hints about what was going on, and she had no reason to suspect him anyway. "I'll meet you all at the gate into the jungle."

"Sounds good."

It wasn't long before Callista and Dathok came jogging up to the gate together. Dathok was taller, a hulking Ocru in black robes that looked very unhealer-like, but Callista was the one who caught the eye. Her gold armor was studded with jewels and shone in the sun. She waved when she got close.

"'Sup?"

Jamie nodded awkwardly. "Hey. Thanks for coming out. I know you probably have more important stuff to focus on than helping a newbie."

"No way," Gracie said emphatically. "We're all just discovering this game, and it's really fun to be poking around in all the zones again. I'm always seeing new things, you know?"

"Yeah." Jamie couldn't help but smile. He'd been enjoying his second run-through for the same reasons. He was focused on leveling up as quickly as he could so that he could be involved in Red Squadron's next month-first attempt, but his new guildmates were encouraging him to really enjoy the process.

After months of playing the game as a full-time job, logging in only for objectives and being graded on them at his monthly employee reviews, this was a welcome break.

It made him feel kind of guilty. He didn't want to like Red Squadron or its guild leader.

"Let's head out and look for some smugglers," Callista suggested. "Dathok, you were with us when we came to the lava place, right?"

"You mean, when we glitched and did some other weird dungeon?" Dathok asked with a laugh.

There was a pause. Jamie perked up his ears.

"Yeah," Gracie said finally. "Long story. So tell me, Cas, how did you get into *Metamorphosis*?"

"A friend recommended it to me," Jamie said, trying to

figure out how to turn the conversation back to the glitch. Callista didn't seem to want to talk about it, and that alone made it interesting.

If there had been a glitch in one dungeon, why not in another? What if their win had been a glitch?

That would resolve this all very easily.

To his discontent, however, Callista steadfastly refused to return to the topic. No matter how Jamie tried to angle the conversation, she always managed to link it to something else…and bring it back around to him.

Nor, he had to admit, was she lacking in strategy. Once or twice, she got them out of situations he was sure were going to wipe the party. If Jamie was looking for evidence that she didn't know what she was doing—and he definitely was—he wasn't finding it here.

But most of all, the party made him laugh. From the Piskie summoner who showed up to the mages who hopped around one-shotting smugglers with fireballs and ice lances and calling out kill tallies to one another, the group was hilarious, and every one of them was eager to help Jamie. By the time he called it a night and headed back to bed, he had to consciously wipe the smile off his face.

He wasn't supposed to like these people. He was going to bring them down from the inside.

CHAPTER EIGHT

Gracie was in the middle of a fight when she felt her phone buzz. She had learned early on that no matter how securely it was wedged in her pocket, it would go flying at some point—and leaving it somewhere else meant that she was missing calls. She'd wound up with a workout armband, therefore, which allowed her to check it pretty easily without worrying she would step on the phone.

She whirled and used her mass-stun before flipping up her headset briefly to check the screen.

Alex. He'd understand if she took a moment before calling him back. She flipped the headset back into place and redoubled her efforts, beating the crap out of a poor harpy who'd done nothing other than be in the wrong place at the wrong time. She had been minding her own business when Chowder ran over to start whaling on her with a mace, and now she and her buddies were deeply outmatched.

Gracie went through the complicated series of strikes

for her most powerful combo, grimacing. Due to the call, she'd used her stun before she'd intended to, and it had thrown off the rhythm of the fight.

For most people, making a bad choice was something they did in the heat of the moment, missing the forest for the trees. For Gracie, though, it took *work* to ignore what she knew was the best course of action, and she could feel the wrongness like an itch.

When she finished the fight, it was with a quick, "AFK." Away From Keyboard wasn't accurate in this game but, by and large, they'd kept the lingo from other MMORPGs.

Panting, Gracie stripped off her headset, pulled her phone out, and called Alex back. "Hey, sorry. I was in the middle of a fight."

"Oh, thank God," Alex said. "I need you to come over soon—like, pretty much now. I spilled coffee all down my pants, and I have that new client coming in again today."

"*Oh.*" Gracie held the phone with her ear and began undoing the rest of the suit. "Okay, so you just need other pants?"

"I don't think any of my other pants are going to go with this shirt very well, so I need a shirt, too. There's a blue one. Wait, maybe the plain white. Or do I want the checked one?"

"Heck, I don't know, dude." Gracie undid one of the clasps with her teeth. "Sec." She held the headset back to her face for a moment. "Hey, I have to run out. I'll be back in an hour or so. You all want me to stay here or port back to the inn?" If the team would be moving on, she didn't want to log back in to find her character being attacked.

"Stay here," Chowder weighed in. "We'll hang out

nearby so we can come to keep you safe while you log in again."

"Cool." Gracie logged out and left the VR suit on the floor as she walked to Alex's room. "Okay, did you figure out which shirt you wanted?"

"I don't knowwww," Alex said. "The checked one? Maybe?"

"There are, like, three checked ones." Gracie scanned the rack. "No, four. Some big, some small, some multicolored, some—"

"You're making it worse!" Alex sounded truly panicked

"Relax! What's the big deal? This guy a super-hardass about fashion or something?" Gracie flipped through the shirts.

Alex snorted. "Pretty much the opposite."

"*Oh.*" It all fell into place. "Oh, I *see.* You have a lunch date, don't you?"

There was a guilty silence from the other end of the phone.

"Uh-huh," Gracie said. "Okay, I'm going to figure out an outfit and bring it, so stop worrying." She hung up without waiting for another word and sighed as she looked at the rack, then she picked out a shirt she figured would set off Alex's eyes, grabbed pants to match, and headed to the door before remembering to get an undershirt, belt, socks, and shoes. "I don't know why men's clothes have to be so complicated," she muttered.

The drive to the office was pleasant but annoyingly bright. Having been shut in the apartment for two days, Gracie wasn't used to the glare of the Las Vegas sunshine anymore.

That, and her skin was getting pale enough to blind people. She looked down at her arms in distaste and wished she hadn't worn a tank top. In fact… She checked her appearance in her visor mirror as she got to the office. Alex worked in a top-tier tax accounting firm, and everyone dressed well.

Gracie, meanwhile, was wearing a tank top with a stain on it, sweatpants, flip flops, and no makeup. She also had clearly not brushed her hair. She scraped it back into a ponytail, gave a sigh, and grabbed the clothes. She couldn't exactly ask Alex to come out to the car with coffee all over his pants, but this was not a great look. Her shoulders were hunched as she walked in.

The woman behind the desk smiled up at her. "Gracie, right?"

Gracie stopped dead. "Uh…"

"Alex said you'd be stopping by," the woman explained. "We met once before."

"Oh. Right." Gracie felt bad. She'd recognized the woman as well but hadn't expected her to remember her name—or know it in the first place. Between that and the other woman's impeccable dress and makeup, Gracie was beginning to wish she could sink through the floor. "Sorry, I was just kind of hoping to, uh…well, not be noticed in this particular get-up." She gestured shamefacedly at her outfit.

The woman laughed as she came around the desk to get the clothes. "If it helps, I'd kill to look that good in sweatpants."

And you're nice, too? Ugh. But Gracie couldn't help but smile. Most people dressed like she was looked down their noses at everyone else. It was nice to meet someone who didn't. "Thanks," she said with a grin. "Tell him I think this'll be a good outfit."

"Will do." The woman smiled, and as Gracie headed for the door, she said, "Mr. Albright, good to see you. I'll be right back."

"Just Harry, please." The man was looking at the receptionist as he answered, so he didn't see Gracie at once. When he did, however, he stopped to stare at her curiously.

Gracie had stopped as well. This was the man she had seen a few times before, with a beard and a shaved head. She hunched her shoulders slightly and gave a nod before heading out to the car.

It was time to go home and shower and put on some real clothes. She felt like a slob.

Unfortunately, her phone rang again—and this wasn't going to be nearly as easy a call. Gracie's shoulders hunched as she answered.

"Hi, Mom."

"Hello, dear." Her mother's carefully cultured voice gave away zero clues as to whether this was a good or a bad call. "I'm so glad I managed to catch you during the workday."

Gracie felt her hackles rise. Her work hours at the casino had been unusual, and it was something her mother had thought reflected poorly on her, missing no opportunities to remind Gracie of what *proper* jobs entailed.

"What's up, Mom?" She knew her voice was abrupt, but she didn't really care. She was not in the mood for this. She was ashamed enough of herself before bringing all of the usual family crap into it.

"I was just calling to ask you if you had plans for the Fourth of July," her mother said.

"Oh. Right." Gracie slumped into the seat of her car and left the door open, her feet out in the breeze. The day was already hot, and the moving air felt good. "What dates were you thinking? Is it like a whole week thing or what?"

This seemed to be the correct question, at least. Her mother launched into a spiel about how they would be renting a house, and people could come and go as they liked. "But you'll want to be here *on* the Fourth, Gracie dear, because that's when Jack is going to propose. It would mean so much to Katie to have you there."

Gracie doubted that. She and Katie weren't particularly close, and in fact, Katie was more likely to be embarrassed by Gracie than happy to see her. If Gracie knew her sister, this was going to be a week of immaculately-groomed people in polo shirts talking about their careers and trying to outdo each other by comparing their favorite wines.

Gracie would spend the whole time she was there dodging questions about what she did for a living and whether she was seeing anyone while Katie, who was on track to be the youngest partner at her law firm, was going to get engaged.

She tipped her head back against the headrest and, to her shame, felt tears in her eyes.

"You know what, Mom? I have to call you back."

"You'll check on those dates, though, won't you, sweetheart? Because we have to know how many rooms we need for—"

"I'll let you know." Gracie hung up and stared at the steering wheel, fighting not to cry. She wanted to call Jay, but the last thing she felt like doing was showing him just how lost and inadequate she was. She would normally go talk to Alex, but everything in his life was clicking along, and she felt guilty derailing his day.

She hesitated for a moment, then searched her contacts and dialed.

"Hey, what's up?" Kevin's voice, without the Piskie filter, was clear and authoritative.

"Do you…have time to talk?" Gracie asked. Her voice sounded very small. "About personal stuff."

There was a pause. "Sure," Kevin said. "Give me a moment." There was a rustle, and in the background, she heard him say, "I need to take this." A few moments later, she heard footsteps and then, "What's up?"

Gracie hesitated.

"Gracie? You there?"

"I…yeah." Gracie pressed her lips together for a moment. "I just feel… I feel… Sorry." Then it all caught up with her and she leaned forward, tears squeezing out of her eyes. "I feel like such a failure right now, and I didn't know who to talk to, and I'm so sorry to dump this on you."

"Whoa, whoa." Kevin sounded concerned. "Did something happen?"

"No," Gracie managed. She sniffled. "Nothing *new*. I just had to go take something to Alex, and I show up and realize I'm in the same sweats I've been wearing for a day and a half, my mom calls about my sister's fucking week-long engagement party—"

"Ugh."

"I know, right? And I *still* haven't told my family what I

do for a living because they were already embarrassed that I worked as a blackjack dealer, and now I play video games, and they won't even *get* that. And it's not like I quit, either. I got fired. For bullshit reasons, but that doesn't make it any better. And I'm single, and I just...ugh." Gracie slumped forward and jumped when she honked the horn. "Sorry. I'm a mess."

Kevin was laughing. "How old are you?"

"Twenty-three."

"Yep, I thought so."

"Excuse you," Gracie snapped, half-annoyed.

"No, I don't mean to...look, what you're going through, it's real, okay? We've all been there. Hell, when I was around that age, I was still the black sheep because I'd just come out to my family, and they turned Alan into the golden child and spent years being nasty to me—"

"You two are *brothers?*"

"You didn't know? Yeah. They tried to pit us against each other, but it didn't really work. Anyway, he ended up not getting married and having kids either, and then they decided we were both disappointments. It's...not important, really. The point is, *everyone* deals with feeling like their career isn't where they want it to be, with worrying that they won't end up where they want romantically, with these bullshit expectations from their family that they know are bullshit but that they can't quite shake. And that's not to write it off, Gracie. I don't want you to feel like I'm minimizing it. It's just to say that, well, you're going to get through this. I *promise.*"

Gracie gave a little laugh. "Thank you. That was exactly what I needed to hear."

"You know, one of my friends' moms liked to say that your life had a bunch of aspects: family, romance, health, career, et cetera. She said that not all of them would be in focus at the same time, and I've found that's true. Sometimes they're *all* out of focus, and it's hard, but it doesn't last forever."

Gracie looked down at herself. Now she felt stupid. She could change her clothes and shower, after all, couldn't she? That would take care of her feeling like a slob. And she *liked* her job. And she could—

Well, she was going to throw up if she thought about the romance aspect of things.

"I can't believe I freaked out," she muttered.

Kevin laughed. "Freakouts are good, right? They tell us we're in the wrong place somehow. For instance, the last time I freaked out, I went and got a way better job. The time before that…well, that was when I realized I had to come out. Right now, I've got a good job and I'm healthy, but things really aren't clicking with finding someone. It's frustrating."

"Yeah." Gracie chewed a fingernail. "Makes me feel a lot better, though, to think of it as a temporary thing, you know? Like, it's not that I'll get everything in place and then things will only go wrong if I screw up, but instead, it's that things will work or not by turns, and I can just expect some chaos in the works."

"Exactly." Kevin sighed. "You sound happier, which unfortunately means I have to go back to writing quarterly reports. Are you *sure* you don't have any more crises for me to solve? Please, anything!"

"My favorite pizza place just closed down," Gracie said promptly. "Can you fix that?"

Kevin laughed. "I'll work on it. See you online tonight?"

"Sure." Gracie hung up and nearly threw her phone in surprise when it immediately started ringing. She answered, "Son of a—hey, no, don't you argue, that outfit will make you look great."

"It's not that," Alex replied. He sounded a bit weird. "Outfit looks fine, thanks. It's, uh…so, that client I mentioned?"

"Yeah?" Gracie decided to stand up and stretch. Her car was by far the most battered and dinged up in this place, and she tried to be amused by that.

"Well, you're never going to believe where he used to work," Alex said.

"Oh?" A second later, her jaw dropped. "Oh, my God."

The man who had shown up very recently, who seemed to be wherever she was. Who had just happened to find himself at her roommate's tax firm.

Who had said to the receptionist…

"Harry," Gracie said. "That was *Harry*."

"I'm coming back in," Gracie told Alex.

"No!" He sounded panicked. "Gracie, you *cannot* come in here. I—shouldn't have told you, honestly. I *can't* tell you stuff like this about clients. I mean…there's a good reason we're not supposed to share client details. Fuck."

Gracie groaned. "No, no, that makes sense. I get it. I won't tell, I promise."

Frustration was coursing through her, though. Even though he hadn't known her before, Harry had turned her into a part of something. A plan for revenge, probably. He'd intruded on her life, and it was annoying as hell that she couldn't confront him about it.

Plus, he'd sought her out. She was sure of it.

That thought made her pause. "Wait. I've seen him around, you know. I saw him at our apartment building, and at the mall, and he *clearly* recognized me when he saw me inside."

Alex said nothing. Gracie knew him well enough by now to picture his brow furrowing.

"I think my point is," Gracie explained, "he's here to talk to me. He'll reach out."

"Oh." Alex sounded troubled. "I just… What do I do?"

Wheels turned in Gracie's head. She kicked at a loose tumbleweed and looked out at the road, where luxury cars were sliding past. She could see a few people looking at her curiously. This part of town was generally filled with people in suits, not sloppy clothes.

Should Alex mention her? Or—

"Nothing. Do nothing." She sighed. "Look, he's trying to be all crazy and make us talk to him instead of just coming out with it and talking to me. He's talking to Jay and he's showing up at your work, and now you and I are trying to figure out what to do? No. Screw that. Just do your job, handle his taxes, and don't spend any time tying yourself in knots over this."

There was a pause. "I like that," Alex said contemplatively. "That would be a *lot* simpler."

"Then let's do that," Gracie said decisively. She got back in her car and turned it on, holding the phone with one shoulder as she put on her seatbelt. "Look, I'm gonna head home. You have a good lunch date, and I'll see you tonight?"

"Yeah."

"What do you want for dinner? I'll order."

"You're awesome," Alex said. "I'm craving something spicy."

"Roger that." Gracie smiled as she backed out. "Talk to you later."

She tapped her fingers on the steering wheel as she drove. Her worries about being sloppy and disheveled had been replaced by more interesting questions. She was even enjoying the sunshine. She rolled down her car window, shook her hair out of its ponytail, and enjoyed the warmth and the breeze. Her hair was going to be a massive tangle by the time she got home, but she didn't care.

At home, she put some water on to boil for pasta and took a shower, putting her hair back in a French braid afterward and donning jeans and one of her nicer shirts. She ate lunch curled up on the couch, staring at her computer and knowing exactly what she had to do.

She just wasn't sure how to do it without getting Alex in trouble.

Jay didn't pick up when she called, but he called her back a moment later. "Sorry. Heard the beep, but needed to log out. You okay? People said you left suddenly."

"I'm fine," Gracie said. "Uh, look. I have to tell you something. I can't explain how I know exactly, but I'd been seeing this guy around lately, and I've found out who he is."

Jay frowned at her. "Is everything okay? Are you…safe?"

"Oh, absolutely." Gracie shook her head then, understanding where he was going with this. She paused. "Uh…I mean, I think so. I don't have any reason to think he would — Well, the point is, it's Harry."

Jay's jaw dropped. "*Harry?*"

"Yeah. I'd seen him at the mall and near our apartment, and then today, I found out who he was."

"How?"

"I can't tell you that," Gracie said uncomfortably. "It's not really important. What's important is—"

"Gracie, *don't* talk to him." Jay's voice was emphatic. He leaned forward in his chair, his brow furrowed. He reached out as if he wanted to take her hand and then pulled back, embarrassed. "Uh, sorry."

"It's okay." Gracie flushed and cleared her throat. "Don't apologize." Did her voice usually sound this weird? She cleared her throat again. "Um. Why *shouldn't* I talk to him? Our plan was to let him come talk to me."

"*Our* plan?" Jay asked.

"Oh, I meant… I figured that would be what you'd tell me to do." Gracie swore at herself internally. She gave a shrug.

"Oh, right. Uh, no, I don't think that's a good idea." Jay sat back in his desk chair, bouncing lightly. He chewed his lip as he considered. "I've been thinking about this lately, and I've been wondering something. I wasn't going to tell you because I wasn't sure if it would make everything worse—"

"Hell, no." Gracie jabbed her fork at him. "Don't start with that."

"You've just been stressed lately," Jay pointed out. "Starting the guild, knowing there might be people trying to spy on us. I feel like the game has become *work*, and part of what makes it so difficult is this quest."

"Maybe, but the last thing I need is people hiding things from me and getting walloped by them later," Gracie pointed out. "It's better to know, even if it feels like a lot to handle."

Jay smiled. "I agree. Well, here's my thought. Question. Thing. I wonder if Harry wanted to be the person who did this quest? If he meant it for *him*, like *he* was going to be the…whatever's at the end of this quest."

Gracie paused with the last bite of pasta halfway to her

mouth. Her mind was racing. All this time, she'd been annoyed at Harry because he'd made a plan that would rope someone else into his revenge. He'd been loitering, trying to find out information about her, and that took a hell of a lot of nerve…

If that was what he was doing.

What if this hadn't been revenge at all? What if Harry had created the quest for himself, and he was trying to figure out what kind of person had tripped it accidentally?

"Oh," she said quietly. And then, "*Oh.* That changes a lot."

"I know it's a lot to handle," Jay said apologetically.

"No, it's *good*," Gracie replied. She took the last bite and chewed. "Thee, it'th—thec." She swallowed. "Sorry. Um, what I mean to say is, this whole time, I hated being this pawn in someone else's game, you know? Like, how dare he make a plan that dragged bystanders in, and how dare he be lurking around and trying to watch me? But what if he never intended anyone else to get caught up in it? That's better."

"Is it?" Jay looked doubtful. "I mean, you're still caught up in it."

"Yeah, but there's no *malice* to it." Gracie shrugged. "That *does* make it different to me."

"Huh. Okay." Jay shook his head. "Sorry I didn't tell you, then."

"No, I get why you didn't. But, yeah, that doesn't worry me." Gracie shrugged and tapped her teeth together as she thought. "Huh. Well, I'm glad I told you, though, because it sounds like he didn't tell you he was doing that."

"No," Jay said slowly. "He didn't. And that's odd."

"It's kind of a weird-ass thing to do," Gracie pointed out. "Maybe he thought you'd tell him it was stalker-y?"

"It *is* stalker-y. Malice or not, it's fucking weird, and I don't like that he found out where you live."

Gracie shifted uncomfortably. "Yeah, me either, honestly. I don't think it's one of those situations that will get super weird, but…yeah. Look, I need to get more food."

"Didn't I just watch you eat most of a box of pasta?"

"Maybe." She gave a shrug. "I'm trying to be 'healthy and budget-conscious.'" She wiggled her fingers with each word. "But I haven't figured out how to fill myself up with home-cooked food yet." She shrugged. "I'm off to raid the kitchen, but I'll sign on soon."

"Okay." Jay waved and waited for her to cut the call.

Gracie wandered over to the window and opened the curtains, squinting against the sunlight. There were trucks moving around at the site for the new buildings. She'd gotten so used to the sounds of construction that she barely heard them anymore.

She opened the sliding door to the porch and leaned against the doorframe, bracing one foot on her other leg.

Life was chaotic. She'd always known that. It was part of what drew her to statistics—the idea of being able to make the best decision possible and know that it would likely come out right in the long run. As much as she had struggled for independence from her parents and teachers, Gracie had accepted the whims of chance with equanimity.

Until now.

Now it felt like she had made one small choice, a choice that should have been next to insignificant, and she'd touched off an avalanche. Beginning that quest had set off a firestorm and made her a leader when that wasn't what she'd been looking for, and now she had a guild to manage, people working *against* her, and she was caught in the middle of a fight that had started long ago.

She'd always known that some things you did had far-reaching consequences, but this was ridiculous.

She sighed, tracing one of the trucks with her eyes as it trundled across the site. This sucked. It sucked, and it was taking everything she had not to run back to her parents. They'd take her in. She knew they would, that was the worst part. She'd start dating a guy they approved of and get a job in an investment firm or something.

It was always there, that pressure. Her childhood had made her acutely aware that there was a model for an ideal child and Gracie didn't fit it. Part of her, she reflected, still believed that it was only a matter of time until she caved and went running home.

"Why not now?" she asked herself. There was nothing holding her here, was there? No boyfriend, no job, no property.

But that was the way her parents would see it, she realized, because those were the only things that mattered to them.

What she *had* was a good friend to live with, a guild full of people who helped each other, and a job she genuinely liked. Gracie had spent her whole life just rejecting what her parents wanted instead of picking her own path. Now she was making her own choices, and she didn't have a roadmap for it.

"It's just going to be scary as hell," she said out loud.

"But it's time to stop wondering if you'll run home. You were never going to do that."

With a small smile, she shut the door and went over to put on her VR suit. She was halfway through when she pulled her phone out and typed a message to her mother.

Hey, I won't be able to make it to Katie's engagement party. Let me know where I can send a gift and a card.

The phone started ringing a moment later, but she ignored the call. She logged in and smiled at the round of greetings.

"Hey, all. Ready to fuck some people up?"

CHAPTER TEN

Alan was the weak link. Jamie figured that out within a few days. The guild's main healer was a smart man, very competent, and very helpful, but he couldn't keep his mouth shut.

After Kevin had mentioned a glitch, Callista must have put the word out that no one was supposed to talk about it. No matter how Jamie pried, he couldn't get a single one of them to tell him about it, and he had long since run out of casual ways to bring it up.

But Alan kept slipping up.

Jamie let the references pass without comment when Callista was there. Sometimes he would interject a question about game mechanics. Sometimes he just wouldn't say anything. He just couldn't let on that he knew something was going on.

He had to pick his time, he told himself. He was anxious; he wanted to be done with this so that his guild could go back to normal. He had to be patient, though.

And then, a few days in, he had an idea.

"Anyone up for cooking?" he asked in guild chat. He'd been keeping track of people's interests, both in-game and in real life. Lakhesis painted Warhammer 40k figurines as a way to make money on the side, Chowder was a surprisingly good golfer, and Freon liked books on WWII military strategy. Callista and Ushanas were the guild's lore readers, always ready to share what they were learning about the zones they explored and the enemies they fought, and Alan? Alan was into crafting. He'd made it an unofficial goal to level in every profession there was in the game, and Jamie had taken note of that.

It was almost too easy. Everyone else made noncommittal noises, but Alan was intrigued.

"I haven't even started that one," he said. "So, if you're cool with me taking some time with the low levels…"

"I haven't started either." Jamie kept his voice innocent. "I heard it was good for buffs, like in WoW?"

"Yeah," Alan said enthusiastically. "Let's go get some supplies. I've got plenty of gold. Meet you in Kithara?"

"I did some research, actually," Jamie said. "In Yantes, there's a vendor who has *all* the supplies, and there's a bunch of fishing we could do." There were auctioneers and vendors in Kithara, of course, but if they were in Yantes, just the two of them, it would be easier to get Alan speaking on a private channel.

"Even better. I'll meet you there."

No one else seemed to notice. "Anyone want to try out combos?" Anders asked. This guild was really obsessed with playing with buffs and debuffs, as far as Jamie could tell. Far from practicing rotations and timing, they seemed to be spending most of their time figuring out who should stand next to whom and which buffs should be activated at the same times.

The more he saw, the more he was beginning to think their run had just been luck. That was going to be a hard sell to his bosses and to Thad, but if it *was* luck, it would be clear pretty soon—when Callista failed to repeat her success.

Alan ported into Yantes a few minutes later and waved at Jamie. His character was a human, short and slender, with long, golden hair that swirled around her in a magical breeze. She reminded Jamie of his own main, the healer he played for Demon Syndicate.

"Okay, I can go buy supplies," Alan said. His voice came through sounding female.

"I had an idea," Jamie said. Now that he was playing a part, everything seemed like an opportunity. "You wanted to fish, too, right? So if you do some fishing, we can get you spices for those recipes, and I'll work on the non-fishing ones. That way, someone in the guild will be able to make all of the recipes, you know?"

"That sounds good," Alan said. "God, it's going to be good having you around. No one else appreciates the crafting. Well, maybe Gracie—Callista, I mean."

"Oh?" Jamie tried to stay calm. Alan was slipping up, and he had to act like he wasn't noticing or the other healer might get careful again. He shoved away a stab of guilt at the idea that Alan wanted to keep him around. As the guild's main healer, Alan had much more of an incentive to want Jamie to go away.

But he didn't seem to operate that way. He'd been eager

to show Jamie all of the spell rotations he used and tricks he knew, some of which had actually been useful. Alan didn't seem to be worried that Jamie would take his spot. He was genuinely happy instead when Jamie nailed a combo or saved everyone's butts on a bad pull.

It both weirded Jamie out and made him feel guilty. This guild was strange.

"You said you did *Dungeons & Dragons*, right?" Alan asked, using the private channel as he bought supplies from the vendor.

"*Shadowrun*, actually," Jamie said. "Why?"

"Callista does a bunch of that stuff," Alan said. "I haven't done D&D in years, or any of that stuff, but you should definitely talk to her about it."

"Uh-huh." Talking directly to Callista was about the *last* thing he wanted to do right now. "How'd you start playing *Metamorphosis*?" People liked talking about themselves. If he could just get Alan rambling away, he'd be golden.

"My brother and I had been playing *WoW* for a few years," Alan explained. "We started back when…well, not important. Our parents haven't been great lately."

"I'm sorry." Jamie's parents were mostly just bemused about his job, but a few people in Demon Syndicate had mentioned that their families were outright hostile about the whole thing. "People get weird about video games."

"It wasn't that, so much as…long story. Basically, we're both huge disappointments." Alan's voice was forcedly cheerful. "So that's Kevin. Fys, I mean."

"Oh. Cool." Jamie hadn't known that. It was kind of difficult to picture the tiny pink-haired Piskie summoner and the golden-haired human woman as brothers, but

Metamorphosis was good for playing mind tricks on people. "Sorry your parents are being jerks," he added.

"Eh, you know how it is." Alan still sounded sad, but he was clearly trying to avoid talking about it. "What about you? You said you'd been playing *WoW* and stuff."

"Yeah, *WoW* and a bunch of first-person shooters." Jamie shrugged. "All the standard stuff. Did some *HotS*, some *LoL*, some *Destiny*. Never really got into any of it. Did raiding for a while in *WoW*, but that's kind of trailed off, you know?"

"Any *FFXIV*?" Alan appeared again with a fishing rod strapped to his character's back. It was a good thing they had magical inventory, Jamie thought, or the tiny healer would be weighted down with bags and bags of flour, spices, and eggs. He opened a trading window as soon as he was close enough and started transferring the different ingredients. "I got us a cooking brazier, too."

"Awesome, thanks." Jamie took the trade and resisted the urge to transfer money back. This character was broke, but his main definitely wasn't, and he felt guilty taking Alan's gold.

He needed to stop feeling guilty ASAP. This man wasn't his friend.

"And no," he added. "I played *FFXI*, and that just wasn't a good one. Before they made some changes, I mean."

"I thought XIV *was* the one they changed."

"No. I mean, they *totally* rebooted that one. XI they just…smoothed down some of the rough edges. But I was gone by then. I heard XIV was good, but I'd heard about *Metamorphosis* and wanted to give that a shot."

"Sure." Alan cast his line into the nearby lake. "This is a

bit different, actually holding your hands out like you have a fishing line. I'm guessing the days of hours-long fishing marathons are done. My arms are gonna be *tired*."

Jamie laughed. He brought up his crafting menu and checked the quests he'd gotten. Five flatbreads was his first quest, and he looked at the icons curiously. Unlike in other MMORPGs, you actually took an active role in crafting. Jamie hadn't been one of the crafters in Demon Syndicate, where everyone split up responsibilities so that no time was wasted.

He had to admit, he was enjoying playing around with the game a little bit.

Smiling, he made the stirring motion to mix the dough, then the kneading motion a few times, and then he placed the dough over the brazier. The cooking surface was magical, a griddle he could only half-see, and it apparently cooked each flatbread perfectly. A few moments later, his inventory icon flared and the flatbread disappeared.

This was kind of fun.

Jamie kept working, mixing the flatbreads and running back to turn in various quests. Yantes was billed as a town that appreciated fine foods, and he and Alan began sharing the funnier quest texts they got, from catering crises to snooty bakers.

"Oh, *fuck* you," Jamie exclaimed, laughing.

"What?" Alan asked. Jamie could just see him on the bridge from here. There was a splash of water from the lake, and Alan's character leaned back, trying to hook a fish that was desperately trying to get away. "No, no, no, no, no! Stay on the line you piece of crap! Nooooo, why? Anyway, what happened with you?"

"Oh, just the same fucking baker who's always getting uppity. 'Well, these croissants are *passable*.' Shut up, dude. You're the one who keeps needing me to cook extra for your business." Jay arrived back at the brazier and shook his fist. "I should take over that business."

"Maybe you should," Alan said, laughing. "Maybe that's the end of the quest."

"I would *love* that." Jamie took out the ingredients for his next pastry. "I cannot get this freaking motion right. What even *is* a *kougin aman*? That's not a real thing, right?"

"Oh, no, those are real. They're delicious, too. All kinda looped at the edges?" Alan caught his latest fish and turned around to watch Jamie. "Okay, so, like this." His character gestured. "You aren't pulling *out* at the corners, you're pinching at the center, two ways, and then it puffs out in four corners."

"*Oh.*" Jamie tried again. This time, he didn't lose his ingredients. "Thanks, I was about to give up and ask if we could trade skills."

Alan laughed. "My arms are *killing* me, so I wouldn't object." He shook his head. "I don't know how the melee fighters do it. Callista and Anders are always just panting like crazy by the end of the big fights. You should have seen the time—"

Jamie hesitated, but he sensed that this was a time when he should push a little. Ignoring a squirm of guilt, he said, "Is this the glitch thing? I know I'm not supposed to know about it, but—"

"Nah, it's…" Alan sighed. "I mean, it's not *really* a secret, it's just this weird thing that tends to happen with Gracie. Gah, sorry, *Callista*. You know who I mean."

"Yeah." He also knew that he didn't want to think of her as Gracie. Finding out about Alan's and Kevin's parents had made all of this a bit more real than he could handle. He didn't want to be thinking about them like they were friends.

"It's just…well, sometimes, dungeons don't quite act the normal way where she's concerned," Alan said carefully.

"Like…you said 'glitching?'"

Alan wavered.

"You don't have to tell me, man," Jamie said. The surprising part was, he meant it. He didn't *want* to get Alan in trouble. He didn't want any of this anymore.

And that genuine reluctance was probably why Alan broke. "It's fine. I'm sure it's fine. I mean, we're just trying not to make a big thing of it, okay?"

"Sure, yeah." *Actually, you know what? Don't tell me.* The words were on the tip of his tongue. He wanted to log out. He wanted to just go back to Demon Syndicate and say he hadn't seen anything.

But he stayed silent. He let Alan dig his own grave and spill the information he wasn't supposed to tell.

"You know that temple overlooking Kithara?" Alan asked. "The old, ruined one with the ice demon in charge of everything?"

"Yeah," Jamie said cautiously. He'd given up paying attention to his *kougin aman* and gave a sudden yelp as they burst into flames. "Crap. Sorry. Uh…" *Use this. Go away. Get more supplies.* "You were saying?" *Dammit.*

"We didn't fight the ice demon," Alan explained. "We went there, and we got through all the beginning mobs, right? And then there was this totally random other boss."

"*What?* That's crazy. So, like, a boss from another dungeon or something?"

"Noooo?" Alan said cautiously. "We looked, and we couldn't find any reference to this guy *anywhere.* Like, he's not a part of the game or something. I mean, he is, clearly. But he wasn't the boss we were supposed to fight there, and there's no mention on the forums that anyone else has run into him."

"That's fucking weird." Jamie shook his head. It *was* odd, and it was clearly an aberration, but he couldn't see how it related to the rest of the issues. "Wait, you said it *tended* to happen?"

"Yeah, it's happened twice more since then," Alan said. "In the lava pit- smuggler area thing, and then in the underground altar-to-the-gods dungeon. Both times we got totally different dungeons, and after the third one, she was in the Top 10."

Jamie stopped dead. "*Oh!*"

The silence went on for too long. He shouldn't have pretended to be interested in that. "Isn't the Top 10 for people in big guilds?" he asked, scrambling to recover.

He could *feel* Alan's relief. "Theoretically, yeah? I don't know. It's been weird. She filed a report with the GMs and all. I guess I don't know what happened with it."

"Huh." Jamie moved the conversation onward, his mind racing. Alan clearly didn't want to talk about this anymore, and Jamie had to keep thinking.

Because this wasn't just about Alan anymore. This was about Callista, and about her finding some strange hack to get the game to give her extra ranking points. Jamie would bet anything that she was just *pretending* not to know what was going on. She was playing dumb, and the rest of her guild was falling for it.

And he was going to take her down.

CHAPTER ELEVEN

Dan had built *Metamorphosis Online*. He had spent hours in the weeds of quest chains, scripts, conditions, and boss battles. He had fallen asleep at night with buff circles exploding behind his eyelids.

But the game had been Harry's dream, and after working on the details for so long, Dan had stopped noticing what the game was even like to play. The details he cared about had been player engagement, social stickiness metrics, and glitch report numbers.

Now, as he strapped himself into a VR headset and got ready to go in, he found himself strangely excited.

He knew that his character stats didn't matter, but he still took his time with the character creation screen, building a male Aosi with greenish-blue skin and black eyes and hair. He rolled as a summoner, intending to deal damage with a bow and have a mortal companion.

When he appeared in the starting zone, he was expecting to find Dhruv with his foot tapping. Instead, he had to wait a couple of minutes before the other founder appeared. To his surprise, when they started a private voice chat, the other man sounded like he was panting slightly.

"That intro was really well done," Dhruv said.

"Oh." Dan frowned. "I skipped it."

"You should reroll," Dhruv said. "It's freaking worth it. Not *now*," he added sharply. "Just later sometime."

"Right." Dan shifted his arms and let the VR suit adjust across his body. He supposed he would get used to it, but it still felt odd. "Okay, explain why we're rolling characters and not coming in with the GM mods?" As GMs, they would have certain advantages like being invisible to mobs and being able to fly. As someone who had never experienced the game content in its final iteration, Dan would have felt more comfortable with that.

"We're retracing her steps," Dhruv said. "And trying to figure out where the next clues are hidden. Is she the only one who can access them, for instance? And what else might he have hidden?"

"She must be the only one who— Wait." Dan frowned. "Jay was the one who found the armor for her."

"Exactly," Dhruv said in satisfaction. "And who knows what Harry would have tagged to avoid our GM keys? Okay, come on."

He led the way up the sloping pathway and Dan followed, bumbling his way into a few corners and occasionally forgetting not to walk on his own. He kept having to stop and pivot rather than walk and turn at the same time, and every time he started again, he took a step forward. It took the glowing red outline of the VR area to remind him, and he was swearing under his breath by the time he realized Dhruv wasn't in front of him anymore.

"Where the hell are you?"

"Backtrack," Dhruv said.

"That's not exactly easy, you know."

"I swear, you are the most unintuitive player I have ever seen. If we had used you as quality control, we'd have the most perfect game ever made…and we'd probably also never finish it. No, stop walking! Look to your right. Your *other* right." Dhruv, despite his frustration, was laughing as Dan turned the wrong way and then pivoted in a dizzying circle. "Do you have the controls inverted or something?"

"Oh. No. And I usually do. That explains it." Dan started trying to bring up menus and was interrupted when his character went staggering sideways, haptics shuddering. There was a snarl and the snap of teeth. "Jesus Christ!"

"Are Americans ever *not* blasphemous?" Dhruv asked philosophically. "No, don't *answer*, fight!"

"I don't know *how* to fight! I don't have a companion!" Dan flailed wildly, trying to hit anything he could, and the wolf shied away from him with a yip as the haptics let him know he'd made contact. He gave a whoop.

"There you go!" Dhruv had thrown himself into the fight, and he managed to beat one of the two wolves backward. "Just focus on that one."

He didn't have time to figure out how to draw his weapon. Dhruv settled into a crouch, pleasantly surprised that his character did the same, and readied himself as the wolf charged again. He punched with all his might and followed up with a kick, and though he overbalanced, the wolf flopped over and disappeared.

"Here, come this way," Dhruv said. "Quickly, before anything else shows up. You're almost dead."

"Crap." Dan tried to follow, walked into a doorway twice, wound up in the corridor again, and finally made his way into the cave. "Follow you into the water?" he asked doubtfully.

"Yeah, it cures you."

"Oh, good." Dan took a step, cursed, and used the walking controls. "Still not used to it. Okay, I'm… Oh, that's good. It gets rid of the red haze."

"Yep," Dhruv agreed. He looked around. "Now, the first quest she did in this chain was after she came out of these caves, so it had to have triggered somewhere in here. Do you see anything? *Anything?*"

"No," Dan said. He pivoted painstakingly and managed to start walking with the controls. "Finally got that right. Okay, the splashing sounds are a nice touch."

"Uh-huh." Dhruv was turning slowly, his Ocru face expressionless. He wasn't really paying attention, Dan could tell.

In his pocket, his phone buzzed. "Ugh, one moment."

"Focus," Dhruv said.

Dan wasn't paying attention. He flipped up the headset, wondering vaguely what was happening with his character's posture, and looked at the screen. When he saw who had emailed, he walked to one of the chairs and sat.

A few seconds later, he heard swearing and Dhruv also flipped his headset up. "What are you doing?"

"Jay emailed," Dan said. He was frowning. "He has a lot of questions."

"Like?" Dhruv sighed. "Our characters are probably getting murdered by wolves right now."

"Good, that'll give me a chance to see the intro when I reroll."

Dhruv gave him a look, leaning down to read over his shoulder. "Hmm," he said contemplatively.

Jay's current email had an energy the others hadn't had. Whereas before, Dan had been talking him into doing things he knew he shouldn't be doing, controlling the encounters with a proverbial carrot on a stick, now Jay seemed to have decided to take the reins. He wanted to know why Harry had made the quest in the first place. He wanted to know what it did. He wanted to know if Harry had intended to be the one doing it.

Alarm bells were going off in Dan's head.

"Knowing Harry," Dhruv said, "that was exactly what he intended. He was going to make himself a god and then boot *us*. Fucker."

"I can't just tell him that," Dan argued.

"Why not?"

Dan struggled to find the words. "He's asking because something *happened*," he explained finally. "The momentum shifted. He has an advantage; he has a piece of information that we don't know."

There was silence while the two men stared at the screen.

"I don't like this," Dhruv said. "I didn't like it to start with, and I don't like it now. What if he's in touch with Harry? He's trying to back us into a corner, and you've given him a really good one. Claiming to be Harry means that—"

"I never claimed to be Harry," Dan said through numb

lips. He'd been very, very careful not to do so explicitly. It was the only thing saving their asses on the legal end.

His phone dinged again and he sighed, intending to ignore it.

Then he saw who had sent the email and he scrolled to it. His heart was beginning to beat double-time. Dhruv read along silently, and a moment later, both of them swore under their breath.

Things had just gotten a hell of a lot more complicated.

Thad was speaking to Evan when Jamie burst into the room. His face was bright. For the first time in days, he didn't look guilty or evasive. He smiled at Thad without a trace of his now-usual apology, and he looked almost savage in his happiness.

"Some big-ass glitch," he said without preamble. "They've been having this weird thing where they go into dungeons and different bosses show up, and since then, *her* rank's been climbing like crazy. They don't know why, and they can't find any mention of those bosses anywhere, but here's the thing…" He now looked so pleased that he had to stop for a moment. He tipped his head back and gave a laugh. When he looked back at Thad, he spoke like he knew he was going to make the leader's day. "They reported it to Dragon Soul. The devs *know* it's a glitch, and they haven't stopped it."

It took Thad a moment to put the pieces together, but when he did, he started laughing.

"Wait," Evan protested. "So they're *helping* her? But if

she reported it as a glitch—"

Thad and Jamie exchanged looks. For the first time in days, they were a united front again. Jamie nodded to Thad to explain.

"He's saying that something went wrong with the rankings, and Dragon Soul has known about it for a while now, but they haven't fixed it. They were trying to help us with the month-first to get us off the trail, maybe, but we have leverage now, because not only did they fuck *that* one up, they didn't tell any of us what was going on. I bet they didn't tell any of the other guilds, either."

Evan looked at them.

"Callista has some weird advantage over all of us in the rankings," Jamie said. "BrightStar is paying Dragon Soul's bills, and they're not giving you a return." His eyes flicked sideways to Thad. *How dumb* is *this guy?*

Thad's mouth twitched. "I'm sure your bosses would like to know about this," he said to Evan.

"Oh. Right." Evan practically ran out the door.

Thad looked at Jamie, both of them laughing for a moment. "You seem happy," he observed.

"We *earned* where we were," Jamie said. He stabbed his finger for emphasis. "*You* did," he added. "And nothing was going our way, and now we know why: it was glitches, and it was Dragon Soul not playing straight with us. We kept *telling* BrightStar it wasn't your fault, and I finally found proof." He rubbed his face. "And now we can just…figure this out and be done with it. They'd better apologize to you."

Thad felt a flush of satisfaction. "BrightStar will make them."

"No, I mean *BrightStar* had better apologize to you," Jamie said. "They've been treating you like shit, and they don't have a clue what they're talking about. You saw Evan just now." He cast an annoyed glance at the door.

Thad crossed his arms. He was cautiously optimistic, but he didn't want to let Jamie off the hook just yet. The other man could have argued for Thad to be doing recon. He could have insisted to Evan's face that BrightStar give Thad an apology.

Thad let the silence stretch, then he gave a small nod. "Let's go see what BrightStar is saying to Dragon Soul," he suggested. He'd set Jamie off-balance, he could tell, and that was enough for now. Jamie needed to remember who'd brought him on board and taught him about the game.

Dan and Dhruv, now out of their VR suits, made sure the door to Dan's office was closed. Dan's finger was poised to start the call to BrightStar.

"Ready?" Dhruv asked. He shook his head. "Remember—"

"*You* remember," Dan said with an unusual burst of prickliness. "Which of us is the one who takes business calls most of the time? *Let me handle this.*"

"Right." Dhruv settled back in his chair and made an elaborate gesture to the phone.

Dan dialed, and it wasn't long until the VP of Bright-Star's media outreach group picked up. Lyle had initially been an easy mark, someone who'd been born in the era of print opinion columns and ads and wasn't entirely sure what *Metamorphosis Online* was. Once they had convinced him that VR gaming was the next big thing, he'd given them a contract that was insanely favorable.

Of course, he'd then gone out and learned everything he could about *Metamorphosis*, and he was now a more savvy investor. That was going to make this call more difficult.

"Hello, Lyle," Dan said. "I'm here with Dhruv."

"Hello," Lyle said. Without preamble, he added, "So what's going on with this? I have the players irate, and frankly, this is reeking of a bad investment. I didn't say anything during the month-first run, but too many twists and turns are a bad sign."

Dan cursed internally. Lyle was right. This *was* getting too complicated, and there was the ever-present fear that things were about to go sideways. Someone would spill the beans, and—

Well, someone already had.

"I think you owe us an explanation," Dan said, "as to how your players have learned of internal glitch reports."

There was a pause. Lyle clearly hadn't expected Dan to come out on the offensive.

"One of our players has been playing within the other guild," he said finally. There was whispering, and Lyle said doubtfully, as if reading aloud, "He rolled an alt." He didn't seem to be sure that what he'd just said were real words.

"Ah," Dhruv said in satisfaction.

"So, *your* players are the ones doing hole-in-corner things now," Dan said. "Is that right? For which *you* were about to hold *us* responsible."

Lyle paused again. "Yes," he said. "But are the reports accurate?"

"That there are glitches in a game of this size?" Dan asked. "Yes. That's why any MMORPG has an entire team of GMs devoted to addressing glitch reports. In a program this large, with this many databases and intersecting elements, there *are* going to be glitches. Now, quite frankly, we offered an unusual boost last month. It worked for us, and given that BrightStar has been exceedingly generous, we thought it only right to make it work for you too."

Lyle said nothing to that.

"However, your players are now misrepresenting themselves in order to get information that *you* are trying to use to gain leverage," Dan said. "I don't like that, and I don't like being blindsided by it. So here's my deal: from now on, we are hooked in when your player is playing with the guild. We get a live feed of the information they're getting, and we can pull the plug at any time. Are we clear?"

There was more whispering.

"Yes," Lyle said finally. Dan could hear protests in the background, but Lyle didn't address them.

"I expect the link to be sent within the hour," Dan said. He ended the call and looked at Dhruv. "Don't get me wrong. I'm not exactly pleased that they're going behind our back, but if they've already got someone well placed, I'd rather use that than not."

Dhruv nodded, and Dan smiled for the first time in what felt like days. He'd been scared for weeks now that Harry had found a way to take the game down.

But they'd dealt with Harry before, and they were going to deal with him again.

CHAPTER TWELVE

"Gracie!" There was a chorus of hellos as Gracie logged in. "Come help us with a dungeon run. We're doing the lava one again."

"The *real* one," Alan quipped.

Gracie frowned. She'd told the team members not to mention to anyone what was going on, but she'd had the sense that it was a losing battle and the truth was just going to leak eventually. Alan, in particular, kept slipping.

Which meant she *really* needed to come up with a plan for when it did.

Eh, she had a little bit of time, didn't she?

"Sorry, guys," she said lightly, "but Jay and I are heading off to explore a bit. Actually…Alan, why don't you come with us? Last time, we had no healer, and it was bad news bears." It would also keep him from running his mouth.

"Then *we* won't have a healer," Chowder interjected.

Gracie checked the roster. "You've got Caspian. Hey, Cas."

"Hey." Caspian sounded hesitant. Gracie had always

gotten the sense that he was a little intimidated by her, which she thought was odd. After all, he was one of the new people who had joined based on her reputation. If anything, she'd expect him to be trying to ingratiate himself with her.

"You up for main-healing a dungeon run?" Gracie asked him.

"I can, uh… I can try."

"You can do it," Alan said encouragingly. "You should see this guy, Gracie. He's a natural. Real good on rotations."

"Well, there you go." Gracie smiled. "Good luck, all, and be nice to the newbie healer. No stupid pulls. Looking at you, Chowder."

"They're not *stupid*," Chowder argued, "they're *ambitious*. I believe in all of you, you see."

"Uh-huh. Well, believe in cooldowns and mana limits next time." Gracie grinned as she saw Alan appear in the middle of the tavern. "All right, the three of us are going to be on a private channel, so just ping someone if you need anything." As Alan walked over, she invited him and Jay to a party. "How's it going?"

"Good." Alan waved. "How are you? Kevin mentioned he talked with you the other day. He was really vague, but it sounded like maybe the whole running-a-guild thing is stressful. You know that's normal, right? Gamers can cause a shit-ton of drama."

Gracie fought down her embarrassment. Kevin hadn't spilled her actual fears, and Alan was offering his support.

"Luckily, I have a good group," she said. "Even some of the newbies are coming along well. But this is all happening pretty fast, yeah. I didn't think I was going to be a celebrity in-game. I just thought I was going to log in, punch some bears, and get shit from my family about my hobbies."

Alan snorted with laughter, one hand coming up to cover his character's mouth. "Yeah, I get that. Hi, Jay."

"Hey." Jay's voice behind Gracie made her turn her head quickly, and she was glad that no one could see her blush in-game.

She emoted a smile. "Hi."

"Hi." He looked at the two of them, then gestured to a table. "Okay, group conference time. Mind me speaking frankly about the Harry thing, Gracie?"

"Ah…" *Not in front of the blabbermouth, please.* But she told herself it was going to come out sometime, anyway. "Why the hell not? Shoot."

"I emailed Harry," Jay said. "I didn't ask him what he was doing lurking around your apartment—"

"Harry's doing *what*?" Alan interjected. "Like, the guy who built the game? He's stalking Gracie? Gracie, have you talked to the police?"

Gracie gave a small smile. "No. Not yet."

"You should." Alan had his character slap the table for emphasis.

"The police are going to ask if he's done anything violent, and then they'll tell me they don't have any cause to charge him with anything. It's just going to be a lot of fuss, trust me. Besides, I don't *think* it's a violent thing. Jay, you were saying?"

"I asked him a lot of other questions," Jay said. "I asked why he'd made this quest, whether he thought he'd be the one doing it, and what his end goal was."

"And?" His tone was frustrated, but Gracie couldn't yet guess why.

"He gave me a lot of nothing," Jay replied, annoyed. "I got through the whole email, and it was like he'd taken a page and a half to say jack shit." He sighed so heavily that his character's body moved. "So, I don't know what to tell you. You know how you didn't like it when he started emailing me? Well, I'm on board with that now."

"Knew you'd come around," Gracie said with a small smile. "And, as it happens, I think *you* were on the right track with thinking he hid some stuff here, so that's what we're doing. We're poking around to find whatever we can find. We're going to figure this zone out: explore every building, every alley—"

"Kill every giant spider," Alan said prosaically.

Gracie shuddered. "At least we know those are there now. I figured we'd start in the inn."

"Good call." Jay had his character stand up. "Top to bottom, or bottom to top?"

"Let's start gentle," Alan voted. "Inn rooms first, spooky basement last."

"You think that's gentle?" Gracie quipped. "You clearly haven't seen the threads on the forums about people RPing in the inns."

"Oh, Lord." Alan dropped his head into one hand. "I should have known."

They made their way up to the second floor, Gracie and Jay cracking jokes about the types of things they might walk in on.

"You think there are Piskie fetishists?"

"What, have you *never* been on the internet before? Of course, there are Piskie fetishists."

"This is so wrong," Alan called up at them.

"Oh, it's all in good fun," Jay said. He opened one of the doors. "No one's actually going to be— *I was wrong.* I was so wrong. Excuse me, I'm sorry."

There was a long, awkward pause while Gracie tried unsuccessfully to muffle her laughter. Finally, she broke.

"Um, what did you see?"

"I'd rather not revisit that memory, thanks." Jay sounded pained. "There were…costumes."

Gracie gave up and howled with laughter. "Okay, we'll start in a different room. See anything else interesting in there? Hidden alcoves? Hidey-holes?"

"Nah, your eye just really goes right to the Ocru in the pink getup." Jay looked up at the ceiling as if beseeching an uncaring god. "I…wow. Oof. That's gonna stick with me."

"Oooookay. Well, we'll try another room. I'll look this time, don't worry." Gracie edged over to the second of the three doors. "Hello? Anyone there?" She pushed the door open cautiously. "Phew, empty."

"You have all the luck," Jay grumbled. "I hope you know how unfair it is. You know—"

"Whoa." Gracie cut him off without meaning to. "Guys, *look* at this place." She walked in, turning around to look at everything. "This is *amazing.*"

The room as good as told the story of Night's Edge, and it gave it a heartbreaking twist. Jewelry and decorations made of shells were present around the room, as were a set of clay figurines in the shapes of merpeople and Aosi. All of them carried weapons, and some had tipped over. A map showed many redrawn lines, indicating an advancing front, and there were sketches of a face that might have been human or Aosi or mer. All that Gracie could say for certain was that the person had been lost and that they were deeply mourned.

There was hope here, too, though. Little human touches, like a carved flute with seashells crudely burned into it. It lacked the distinctive elven grace of the Aosi or the actual sea materials of the merpeople, but whoever had owned it had treasured it for its attempt to pay homage to the sea.

The window on the far wall looked out over the bay, and Gracie found herself wondering if the person who lived here used the view as an inspiration or a reminder of what had been lost.

"What are you thinking?" Jay asked quietly.

"That life goes on," Gracie said slowly. "That people find a way. Here's this flute, this sign that humans are here, trading, living. There's a friendship here, something beautiful and strong, but it never would have happened without the war. Night's Edge now is built on that rubble." She looked at him, eyes searching his face even though she knew it was only pixels and not really him. "Sometimes Harry infuriates me, but sometimes I see this vision of the world he wanted to show and it's hard to be angry."

Jay was silent for a moment. Alan had crouched to look at the figurines.

"Can I ask you something?" Gracie said to Jay.

"Sure."

"Where do you think this is all going?" Gracie asked him. "He built this quest...we think. But we don't know why, and we don't know what's going to happen at the end. I think that's a big part of what's stressing me out. I love this place, Jay. I love it so much, and I don't think Harry would do something that would destroy it, but what if I'm wrong? I didn't know him, and it kind of sounds like he was an asshole."

"He was. He definitely was." Jay chewed his lip. "It's hard to explain. Um. To tell the truth, I don't *know* where this is going. I wish I did, Gracie. That's part of why I'm trying to figure it out. I want this shitstorm to be over with."

"What if it just gets *worse?*" Gracie burst out. She sighed. "I'm sorry, but we should think about it, shouldn't we?" She was aware of Alan hovering awkwardly.

"We'll figure it out," Jay said. "Every time I think I understand this, you say something like what you said about the flute, and I remember that Harry wasn't as simple as we wanted him to be. He wasn't *just* an asshole, Gracie. I think you see something in this game that he wanted everyone to see. And I think you're right: he wouldn't destroy it all."

"Ugh." Gracie sniffled and then rubbed her stomach. "And now I'm hungry. I'm going to order something, I'll be right back."

"Good call. We'll poke around the inn—well, depending on what's lurking in these rooms. Just join us whenever you're back."

"Roger that." Gracie sighed as she took off her VR helmet. She could see Alex's shoes at the door. "Yo, Alex."

"Hey." His voice echoed down the hall.

"I'm ordering dinner. What do you want?"

"Can't." He walked out into the main room, putting gel in his hair. "I have a date."

"You had a lunch date," Gracie said.

"Yeah, and it went well." He gave her a grin. "Until we ran out of time, so…"

"Ew, staaaahp! I don't want to hear about it." Gracie stuck out her tongue. "Go on, go on, have fun. I'll order something just for me."

"You should try Giacomo's," Alex suggested. "It's what went in when Carmelita's closed down. Don't give me that face. It's good pizza, too. Carmelita's is closed, Gracie. Your loyalty gets you nothing."

"If you stand on principle only when it's easy, you betray yourself." Gracie shook her fist. "I would rather eat gravel. I'll get Thai food or something. Have fun on your date."

"I intend to." Alex slipped his shoes on, gave her a last grin, and practically ran out the door.

Gracie chuckled and rolled her eyes as she dialed the number for the Thai place nearby. She had only just ordered when a knock sounded at the door and she frowned.

"That was absurdly quick—" she began as she opened the door.

But it wasn't her takeout. It was Harry.

CHAPTER THIRTEEN

Gracie hadn't intended to get freaked out, but Alan's words came back to her: *Harry is stalking you?* She opened the door. She saw Harry. She slammed the door.

Directly in his face as he'd stepped forward.

She heard the door slam into his head and clapped a hand over her mouth. Wrenching the door open, she was confronted by the sight of a tall, bald, bearded man with his hands over a bloody nose.

"I'm so sorry," Gracie managed. "I'm *so* sorry."

"What the fuck?" Harry asked, his voice muffled. "You just slam the door on me?"

Gracie had been sorry a moment earlier, but Harry's anger touched off her own. Her eyes narrowed. "Excuse me?" she asked, her voice icy-cold. "You follow me around for a week—*at least*—show up at my door, try to step inside without being invited, and get mad at *me* for shutting the door on you? Are you fucking kidding me?"

Harry stared at her. His hands were clasped over his nose, and blood was trickling out from beneath them, over his lips and chin. As surprised as he was, this might be the first time in his life that anyone had ever yelled at him. Gracie crossed her arms and gave him what Alex called the Look-with-a-capital-L. She smiled her customer service smile, the one that said, *I have to be nice to you on the surface, but I'd shank you in a second if I could.*

She waited.

Finally, Harry said. "Can I have a tissue or something?"

Gracie raised an eyebrow.

"Fine," Harry snapped. "I'm sorry. Was that what you wanted to hear?"

"Yes," Gracie said. "I'll go get you a tissue. Ah, ah, ah," she added, as Harry stepped forward. She closed the door, locked it, and went to go get a tissue. When she came back, it was to find him waiting with a manifestly unimpressed expression on his face. "You show up unexpected at people's doors, dude, you take what you get."

He wiped his nose carefully, taking tissues from the proffered box and cleaning himself up. Then he looked up at her. "May I come in?" His voice was a parody of courtesy.

So, apparently he had learned nothing. Gracie considered just saying no and shutting the door in his face, but she had questions she wanted answered.

"Why?" she asked, instead.

"Because we're on the same side," Harry said, through gritted teeth. This was definitely a man who was used to having people fawning over him.

"What side?" Gracie asked innocently. She tilted her head. "I don't even know who you are." When he glared, she gave a smile. "Am I supposed to?"

"Your roommate told you exactly who I am," Harry said.

"Don't think so," Gracie said. "He's very private about his work. Are you a colleague?"

Harry gave her a look. "Fine. Your roommate didn't tell you. I get it. But you know who I am, and you *know* we're on the same side, so let me into your damned apartment."

"Your chances are going down," Gracie informed him, "not up. You may be used to people who go running when you start to talk loudly and get all threatening, but I've been working in a casino, buddy. I've seen professional football players drunk off their asses and wanting to fight anything that moves. I've seen security guards practicing all the moves to look big and scary. You want to bluster and shout at someone when they have the audacity to call you on your bullshit? Well, guess what, that's not going to get you anywhere with me."

From the look on his face, Harry wanted nothing more than to storm off down the corridor and leave. The fact that he didn't showed just how badly he needed her, Gracie thought. He gave her a look of open dislike.

"Why me?" Gracie asked him. "It was random, wasn't it? It had to be. There's no way you would have known who I was before all this started."

He gave a curt nod.

Gracie gestured for him to keep going. She wasn't going to fall into the trap where she interrogated him. She might ask the wrong questions, and Harry was *definitely* the type of person not to tell her if that was what she was doing. She had to let him talk. Then, he'd tell her the real story. People were uncomfortable with silence.

When she said nothing, he gave a sound halfway between a sigh and a growl. "What do you want from me?"

"You showed up at *my* door, buddy. You don't get to talk to me like that." Gracie narrowed her eyes.

Then the dam broke.

"Do you have any *fucking* idea what you've done to my life?" she demanded. "Literally, the first fucking clue?"

Harry said nothing, His nose was leaking again, and from the way he was twitching his lip, he knew it. But he didn't seem to dare reach for another tissue.

"I was just trying to play a goddamned *game*," Gracie half-shouted. "I got a VR set because my roommate said I would like it. I rolled a character with blue skin because why the hell not? I'd always wanted to be an elf, and you know what? I fucking *loved* it. It was a beautiful world, it was a *beautiful* story. There was love and there was loss, and I was fighting for things that mattered and working for peace. Instead of *having* that, now I have all this other bullshit to deal with!"

One of the doors down the hall opened, and a guy stuck his head out the door. "Hey, do you *mind*?"

"Sorry," Gracie said. She grabbed Harry's arm and yanked him into her apartment, slamming the door behind him.

"I'll explain," Harry said curtly.

"NO. You'll fucking *listen*, you piece of shit." Gracie threw up her hands. "Okay, that was slightly over the line."

"Slightly?"

"Yeah. Slightly." Her face dared him to argue with her. "My life wasn't great, all right? I had a shit job, my family was always on my damned case, I didn't have a boyfriend.

What I needed was for something to distract me. I needed to have a place where I could chill out with friends and feel like I was fighting for something. Do you get that? Do you even…" She waved her hands. To her horror, there were tears in her eyes.

Harry said nothing for a moment. His arms were crossed over his barrel chest, and he was staring at the ground.

"It wasn't supposed to be you," he said finally. "It was supposed to be me."

Gracie wiped at her eyes. "Why a quest, then? Why not just roll a character with those abilities?"

"Because I saw the writing on the wall," Harry said. "They were forcing me out, and I knew it. They could block my ability to get into the game, roll a GM character, change a few access codes or leveling mechanics, and I'd never be able to get my powers back. But I wove the quest in. They weren't looking for it, they were never going to take it all out. Doing the quest would…" He shook his head. "Make me a god. In the game."

Gracie stared at him for a long moment.

"And then *you* did it," Harry said unnecessarily. "And only one person can do it."

Gracie swallowed. She looked down at the floor, biting her lip, and tried to think of what to say.

"Why?" she asked finally. "What was even the end goal? To be a god, you said that, but what does that mean? And *why?*"

"It's not important," Harry said.

"No, it *is*. Because I'm stuck in this now, don't you see?" Gracie shook her head. "I have people trying to infiltrate my guild and take me down as an example because I won some ranking contest I didn't even fucking care about?"

"Yeah, I don't know what's going on with that." Harry scratched his beard. "I didn't intend to have it affect the rankings. Must be a glitch."

"I swear to God, if another one of you fucking people mentions glitches, I am going to start punching people in the throat," Gracie gritted out. "I don't care whether or not you *intended* it to cause the rankings issue."

"A moment ago, you said you did." Harry gave her the same bland customer-service smile she'd given him.

"Remember what I said about punching people in the throat?" Gracie asked him. "Because you're getting there. I want to know what you intended, but I also want you to know just how much you fucked my life over."

"I'm given to understand that you now play video games for a living," Harry said bluntly. "That place on the rankings pays a lot of money each month. And don't tell me you liked working in a casino."

Gracie stepped over to the door and opened it. "You explain how you know so much about me, or you leave," she said. Her lips were numb.

Harry rubbed his face. "Should I just go?"

"If you're going to be a superior son of a bitch who isn't helpful, then yes," Gracie snapped. "I have the Dragon Soul game developers mad at me for nothing I did, I have a bunch of companies whining about how I jacked the ratings, I have a bunch of bullshit to keep managing, and all I freaking wanted was to let off some steam and play a game. If you want to be *another* source of drama, you can get out. If you want to explain what's going on, you can stay."

Harry sighed and leaned back against the wall, his hands in his pockets. He blew out a breath.

"Here's the thing no one else understood," he said. "The game is *real.*"

"Beg pardon?" Her voice came out sounding way too much like her mother's. Gracie cleared her throat hastily.

Harry shook his head in frustration. "You remember what I said to you at the altar? No action is wasted. What you do, how you behave—that becomes a part of you. It ripples back into the real world."

"That *was* you?" Gracie shook her head. "How did you get in?"

"I made a character!" Harry shouted. "To make you lose the quest!" When he saw Gracie's expression, he groaned. "If I could make you fail it, I could pick it up," he said, through gritted teeth.

"And I beat you." Gracie was starting to smile. She didn't want to rub it in, not necessarily.

But she *did* like winning.

"Yes," Harry said. He clearly wasn't happy about this turn of events. "You did. Good for you."

"Sorry. Well, not very, but you see what I mean. It's just, after you've fucked with my life a ton and given me this giant pile of frustration, it's kind of nice to see you get a dose of it too." Gracie grinned at him and leaned against the other wall, crossing her arms. "Go on."

He gave her an unfriendly look. "You didn't back down," he said. "You never took the out. You wanted to fight for something more, for the right thing, whether or not it was easy. *You* understood. You couldn't just watch an injustice happen and walk away, even in a game."

Gracie shrugged.

"You don't get it," Harry said. "Dan and Dhruv thought I was nuts. They said it was just a game, they said people got to learn their limits and test out things they would never do in the real world, but when you make a dystopia, when you make people start to choose between amoral options, when they get used to it…that can do more harm than you could imagine."

Gracie frowned at him. "Not sure I buy that. I've made some bad choices in games, regretted them, and come out the other side with the impetus never to do that again."

"You're different," Harry argued. "That's why you triggered the quest. No one else had, and there were already thousands of players."

Gracie chewed on her lip. Harry sounded frustrated, like he was absolutely sure of his conclusion, but she wasn't sure she agreed.

"Okay," she said finally, noncommittal. "So why did you come to see me?"

"Because I wanted to know who you were." Harry lifted his shoulders and shook his head. "This was supposed to be my way to stay in the game. Do you know what it's like, dreaming up something like *Metamorphosis*, and then it becomes *real,* and there's no place for you there? Do you have any idea? Because I made my place, and you have it."

Gracie stared at him, shaking. In her head, she'd called Harry a lot of names. She'd thought badly of him for messing with her life, for making her a pawn.

But she also knew what the game meant to her, and she couldn't even imagine what it meant to him.

"I'm sorry," she said quietly. "You did a good job, you know."

Harry gave a single shake of his head. "I don't want to hear about it." He looked away for a moment. "What I want to know," he said finally, "is that you'll do what I made that character to do. That you'll make sure they don't slide into chaos and backstabbing. That you'll keep them on the right path."

"Them?"

"All of them." He met her eyes. His were brown, set beneath thick dark-blond brows. "The players."

"I…how the hell am I supposed to do that?" Gracie demanded.

"Figure it out," Harry said. "You were the one who cared enough to save the kobolds, and they aren't even real. So you should care more about actual people, right? Figure it out." He gave her a look that was not entirely friendly and left.

Gracie stared after him, her head whirling. She hadn't expected to sympathize with Harry, not at all.

And she definitely hadn't expected him to give her an even more impossible task than she already had.

CHAPTER FOURTEEN

"I still don't know why they agreed," Thad was saying heatedly as Jamie got into his VR suit. "We don't owe them a damned thing. *They* owe *us*—"

Jamie lost Evan's reply as he put on his helmet. Thad was probably looking for backup in this fight, but Jamie didn't want to take the time and frustration for that. Evan wasn't the person they should be arguing with anyway. *That* would be whoever had agreed to a livestream.

And even that wasn't really on his radar.

Callista was.

While they were all descending into accusations and in-fighting, Callista was taking her ranking to the bank. She was making herself an icon in the world of *Metamorphosis*. Everyone loved a damned underdog story, didn't they? And here she was, running away with the title without a sponsor. She was probably beating the advertising offers away with a stick by now. It made Jamie's chest feel tight. Hot, and filled with anger.

She'd made a mockery of the rest of them, and he would bet she didn't even care.

He loaded into the middle of a guild conversation that sounded anxious. The members of the guild were practically whispering to one another, a human urge that hadn't quite caught up to the fact that they were in a virtual world.

"What's going on?" Jamie asked. He'd loaded in near Kithara, in one of the fields that had a reliable scattering of herbs. As he progressed in his cooking, he was going to need more ingredients, and while he hoped he was almost done with this farce, he did need *something* to do in the meantime. He headed for one of the small lakes that dotted the landscape.

"Hey, Cas." Alan sounded somber. "Something weird is going on with Gracie. I don't know exactly what. She and Jay are talking about it."

"I hope everything's all right." What he *actually* hoped was that his voice didn't sound too happy. Had all of this finally caught up with Callista?

He could only pray.

To his manifest frustration, however, no one knew anything more, and it was more than two hours before Callista emerged from her closed-door session with Anders. By then, most of the other guild members had logged off, and Jamie was beginning to think that tonight wasn't a good night for getting any intel. He wondered, amused, if the Dragon Soul devs were still watching or if they had given up.

And then it was only the two of them online, and he felt

the adrenaline start to kick in. This was it. He was going to bring her down, make her give all the details.

Slow and steady, Jamie. He bounced on his feet, trying to burn off the extra energy. His character was collecting herbs to use in cooking, and he sank back into the shadows as a pair of wolves padded by.

"Hey," he said to Callista, knowing that the wolves couldn't hear him but still feeling a spike of adrenaline. "Up late too, huh?"

"Yeah." Callista sounded exhausted. "I should sleep, but I just…I can't."

"Are you all right?" Jamie asked as innocently as he could. He stepped out of the shadows and made for a bunch of herbs near the lake. "Everyone was really worried."

Callista swore under her breath. Jamie made out "monkey-brained" and "canoes up their asses" and decided not to try to put the pieces together.

"Sorry," she said, after a moment. "It was just, that was exactly what I *didn't* want."

Of course. You don't want to be the center of attention. You don't want to milk this for all it's worth. Jamie felt his lip curl. He'd been starting to get tired, but this was energizing him. "They're just worried about you," he said. "They care about you." He'd stroke her ego and see if that got him in her good graces.

"Right." Callista sounded like she was trying to be happy but wasn't managing it particularly well.

There was silence, then she said, "Thanks for helping out with the cooking, by the way. You made Alan's week, I swear." She sounded a bit happier now. "He's been on our case to learn to craft, and no one's taken him up on it. It'll be nice for him to have a buddy."

"He's a good dude," Jamie said honestly. "Which is a weird thing to say about a tiny blonde chick."

Callista gave a full-throated laugh. "Don't I know it! This game messes with people's heads. I thought Alan and Kevin were women for a while there, and *they* all assumed I was a dude, which was hilarious. Lakhesis actually is a chick, if I remember correctly, and I have my suspicions about Dathok."

"I can't tell if it's better or worse than *WoW*," Jamie said. "Because there's the voice-filter thing, so it really feels like you're getting to know them. Then you remember, 'Oh, right, no one has a built-in echo in their voice.'" He waded into the water, making for a small island, and disappeared under the water when the ground fell away sharply. He shut his mouth by instinct, his throat seizing up, and thrashed…

And then remembered he wasn't actually underwater. It was hard to force himself to breathe, though.

"You okay?" Callista asked.

"Just fell into a lake while looking for herbs."

"Oh, I'll come help you gather. That'll level my gathering, too. Sec." She sent a party invitation, and he saw the ether symbol appear next to her name in the guild list, indicating that she had teleported.

"You don't have to help," Jamie said awkwardly.

"I don't mind. Actually, it'll be nice and calming. I'm worried that if I try to do anything combat-ish, I'll throw my back out. It's been a *day*, let me tell you."

It was a couple of minutes until Jamie saw her running

through the tall grass. Her usual bright golden armor had been replaced with a gathering outfit, a long tunic in a singularly unflattering shade of brown, sandals, and a wide-brimmed straw hat. He gave her a thumbs-up.

"That's a good look."

"Sewed it myself," Callista said, returning the gesture. "I can feel my Aosi forebears turning in their graves. I'm sure a *proper* Aosi doesn't leave the house in anything less than black tie."

"Sounds about right." Jamie had never been a huge fan of the Aosi. He didn't usually like elves, and the Aosi had all the qualities that made him roll his eyes: height, good looks, smug superiority, and long lives. It didn't seem the least bit interesting to him. "Why'd you choose an Aosi?" he asked, waiting to hear her say that she'd wanted to be graceful and elegant…or stammer something out about how she wasn't quite sure.

"I wanted to be blue," she said after a moment of musing. "The more I see of them, though, the more I like it. I keep playing around with backstory in my head, you know?"

"How so?" Jamie hopped up on a rock and went sliding back down. It was just like the times he'd spent climbing outcroppings in other video games, but here he got a jolt in his haptics every time he fell.

"I love elves, usually," Gracie said. "I don't think writers do much with them, though. What I like best about *Meta-morphosis* is that it really drives home that they *aren't* all high and mighty, right? Like, they were made to be these superior beings, but they made the same mistakes as everyone else."

"Huh." Jamie considered this. "So you like that they're...normal?"

"Yeah." Callista's character shrugged. She was also hopping up the embankment, trying to get to a different clump of herbs. "Oh, son of a bitch, I really thought I had it that time." She landed with a little puff of dust, one of the incongruous things about the game world. No matter where you were, you landed with dust puffing up.

"So, not like Tolkien elves," Jamie said after a moment.

"No, I think they're pretty much like Tolkien Elves," Callista said. "Think about it—the elves also fell prey to the rings of power, they also have infighting and gross people in the ranks, and they die in battle. They look down their noses, but it's really nothing more than any other faction dispute. They just dress it up in what *sound* like good reasons."

"I suppose," Jamie said doubtfully. "So, then my question would be...sec." His character picked the herbs, and he gave a whoop when a rare-quality one appeared in his inventory. "Oh, *hell* yes. I'll finally have a shot at making roasted antelope. It needs *rare* oregano or no dice."

"Who knew it was so finicky to cook?" Callista asked whimsically.

"You should have seen the *kougin aman*. I wasted eight batches of dough in a row before I figured out the hand motion. Anyway, sorry, I was going to ask, why did you start thinking of elves that way? And why would you want to play one, if that's how you think of them?"

"I don't know. I guess it just reminds me that people are people. You can think you're above everything or you're better, but no amount of smarts or good looks or riches or anything will keep you from experiencing all of the hard stuff."

Jamie blinked. He worked in silence, turning that over in his head.

"Not that I wouldn't like to have the chance to *prove* that money doesn't buy happiness," Callista added.

That snapped him back to himself. She was trying to cheat other people out of their money. Of course, she was focused on it.

"What was your job before this?" Jamie asked. "I mean, you do *this* now, right?"

"Yeah. And it's not all it's cracked up to be, I promise." She shrugged. "Though I expect saying that is like a rich person saying that being rich isn't so great, huh? I don't mean to be rude. It just all happened very suddenly. I was a blackjack dealer before this."

"And then your rank started to climb, and—"

"No, it wasn't the game. Well, it kind of was." She stopped, and he heard her blow out a sigh. "This is going to sound weird. Basically, the game gave me a spine."

Jamie looked at her. "I, uh…"

"I got told to do something at work, and it wasn't the right thing to do. Before starting *Metamorphosis*, I probably would have just knuckled under. I was used to doing that you know? Having other people run my world for me, and —huh."

Jamie waited. When she said nothing, he prompted. "Huh?"

"I just, uh…just put something together. Can I ask you something? A—friend—and I were having an argument about the game. I wonder which side you come down on."

"I'd rather not get involved in arguments." Lord knew he had enough of that in his life right now.

"It's more of an opinion question. I don't think there's a right answer. And I won't even tell you whose side is whose. Basically, one of us thinks that the game is a good place to try out things you'd never do in real life because it means you get to experience regret and learn where your limits are morally, and the other one thinks that how you behave in the game is directly *parallel* to how you behave in real life. So, if you start doing immoral things in the game, you'll start doing them to other people too."

"I'd guess you're the person who thinks they're parallel," Jamie guessed, "given what you just said about how you've changed. And I don't know. I could go either way. I did two run-throughs of Mass Effect, one on *Paragon* and one on *Renegade*. Other than being bored as fuck playing *Paragon*, I don't think I changed much as a person."

"Hmm." Callista considered this. "Want to try that hill over there? My mini-map says there's a ton of stuff."

"Sounds good."

"And I was actually the other one," Callista explained as they waded into the water and swam to shore. "But now that I describe what happened, I realize maybe my friend is right. I don't know."

"Like you said, it's an opinion question," Jamie pointed out. "You're probably both right. Who were you arguing with, Anders?" He grinned. "Was that what the big two hours away was all about? You were actually talking philosophy?"

Callista burst out laughing. "Yep, that was it. Went to

get dinner, had a big serving of ennui, and came back to talk Kant and Aristotle."

Jamie snorted. "You guys live it up around here."

"I don't want to say we're the *coolest* cats," Callista said. "But we pretty much are. I don't want to brag, but last night I had caffeinated tea after dinner."

"Look, I don't mind hearing about your depravity as long as you keep it private," Jamie said, pretending to be prim. His mouth was twitching, though.

What was *happening*? Was he actually starting to *like* this woman?

"Uh, so you didn't do the thing at work?" he asked.

"Ugh, yeah. I quit before they could fire me. We sort of had to make the month-first after that for me to make my rent. Let me tell you, we did *not* think we were going to pull it off."

I'll bet the rest of them didn't, at least, Jamie thought sardonically. "Oh?"

"It's been a weird few weeks," Callista said with another shrug. "Frankly, having a bunch of new people coming on board is sort of stressful all on its own. But I'm glad you're here, really. Please don't take that the wrong way. I'm just super-awkward."

"Bet you're happy being number 1," Jamie suggested.

"Not…really?" Callista sighed. "Don't get me wrong, it *is* nice to be able to make rent. It really is. I don't want to be ungrateful. It's just, well—I don't know if anyone's spilled the beans yet, but we might as well. There's been this weird thing happening with some of the dungeons, and I honestly don't know what's going on with my rank. There's a bug report open, so we'll see what happens."

"Huh." Jamie hadn't expected her to admit that.

"I wish they'd just get back to me," Callista said. "But it is what it is. I'm sure they're just trying to figure out what to do, you know?"

"Right." Jamie thought of the conference calls, the tip-offs about the month-end raid, the spying they were doing, and he felt another unexpected pang of guilt.

He shoved it down deep. He wasn't going to get taken in by this act, he promised himself.

CHAPTER FIFTEEN

"All right, Altar of the Gods, Round 2." Gracie squared up and rolled her neck. She and Jay had come to the conclusion that they should redo the original steps of the quest in order to learn more about Harry's goals and motivations and predict where the next steps might be found. So far, no additional pieces had come open, and Gracie wasn't feeling good about asking Harry.

She hadn't told him yet, but her hope was that redoing this stage would give her a chance to throw the quest. Fail intentionally, and then have Jay remove the starting condition so that Harry could never begin it.

She didn't think she wanted the quest to exist. It wasn't that the idea of being a god didn't appeal—in fact, it appealed a *lot*—but Gracie wasn't sure she should have that kind of power. And despite the fact that Harry had created this world, she was *very* sure that *he* shouldn't have that kind of power.

Jay was *not* going to like this.

She shook her head and refocused. She would deal with that later.

"Everyone, remember to be nice," Alan said. "We have Cas on board as backup healer, so let's not make this a terrifying experience for him."

"Really, I'm fine." Caspian sounded a bit prickly, and Gracie smiled. She often got the sense that Caspian was being very reserved, and it was always nice when a bit of his true self peeked through. In this case, she completely understood the feeling of being annoyed when people tried to go easy on her.

"I'm with Cas," Dathok rumbled. "This is my first time running a dungeon as DPS, so let's pull *everything* and see where it goes."

Gracie snorted. "Man, when healers go bad, they *really* go bad. Someone keep an eye on Dathok and make sure he doesn't go entirely to the dark side."

"On it," Chowder said.

Jay leaned over to Gracie. "We're doomed," he said seriously.

Gracie snorted. "All right. Now, if I recall correctly, the first parts of the dungeon went the normal way, right? We fed the altars, then fought the various demon whatsits that appeared?"

"Yeah."

Gracie bounced on the balls of her feet. Now that she was actually thinking of dropping the quest, her heart was racing. "I want to try something new this time." Her voice sounded weird in her own head. She could only hope the voice filter masked it.

"Oh?" Everyone looked at her.

"You mean, other than having a new alt healer and having your old alt healer be a rogue?" Dathok clarified.

Gracie forced a laugh. "Yeah. I'm going to try generating threat a bit differently. I had a hunch about some combos that might work."

In reality, she was sure that all of the combos she was dreaming up would fail miserably, and it was going to be hellish to spend the whole run doing the exact wrong thing. It was like someone dragging their nails down a chalkboard.

But it would set her up perfectly to lose when the boss showed up. She swallowed, nodded to herself, and got ready.

By the end of this, she was going to be just another normal player. Her rank would go back to normal, and she'd have Jay erase the quest and tell Harry to resolve his differences with Dan and Dhruv in some other way. She wouldn't have lost anything, she told herself. Not really. She'd just have to go back to having a job.

A shitty job dealing blackjack.

Spending time with coworkers who looked at her funny when she talked about video games.

Without waiting any longer, she started to run toward the first altar. If she was going to do this, she should just do it. As she ran, she let her mind drift. It was her personal belief that Harry had set the pieces of his quest in the zones and encounters that meant the most to him out of all the game lore, so why had Harry put part of the quest here in this dungeon?

This was a place where the gods had come to worship, and they had perpetrated all manner of cruelty in order to do so. Gracie almost wondered if their sacrifices hadn't been so much warm, living bodies as entire wars, famines, and plagues.

Was Harry making a point to himself about the perils of power? About how even gods would inevitably look for more and sink into depravity? Or was he just making a ham-handed point about Dan and Dhruv? Gracie rolled her eyes. With Harry, it really could be either.

The problem was, she got a sense that if he weren't so used to people rushing to placate him, he would probably be a pretty cool person to hang out with.

The first enemy appeared—a figure they could barely see, twisting in agony over the pristine white altar. It shrieked at all of them, *"You refuse to give the sacrifice?"*

So far, the same. Gracie held her position as the rest of the party fanned out to surround the altar.

"Then I will choose from among you."

This time Gracie didn't bother to correct it. She rushed it, luring it down with a flurry of smaller attacks and beginning an unusual rotation. She felt herself slipping into her usual combos, always wanting to build threat with her tried-and-true methods.

But she had to sell this. She had to make them buy it, so instead, when she felt the itch of wrongness in her head, she went toward it.

Last time she had done a very specific set of combos, burning the boss down with quick DPS, using Freon's magic to root it in place while it did an AoE spell, and then doing the last portion of the burn. This time she didn't burn it down as quickly, and she realized that its AoE was on a timer, not tied to the levels of its life. That meant they had to go through the process of dancing out of range over and over again, and each time, someone or other would take a fair amount of damage.

She let herself get lost in the fight. She would lay down a few attacks, then let the others circle in. Dathok was replacing Alex tonight, his stealthy crouch hilarious in something the size of a male Ocru. Fys sent arcane bolts whizzing through the air, her fire demon roaring and slashing at the god on the altar. Jay was practically a blur, compensating for Gracie's changed attacks with different ones of his own.

Gracie tried not to feel guilty. He wasn't asking her what was up even though she wasn't up to her usual standard. She wanted to tell him what she was really doing.

But he would try to talk her out of it.

She also realized just how long this was going to take if she kept fighting so poorly. She was used to the fights already being over, and between Dathok being new to DPS and Gracie failing to hold threat, this was taking significantly longer than usual. Gracie watched the boss's health bar creep down, trying to lose herself in the muscle burn.

She couldn't let them wipe yet, so she ended up drawing the fight to a close with a few of her usual combos.

As they paused to regain their health, she felt an unexpected surge of anxiety, looking at the relatively short time left on the dungeon clock. It just felt *wrong* to play this way.

It was Alan who contacted her privately, his character looking in the other direction so that no one would guess they were talking.

"Everything okay?" he asked cautiously.

"Yeah, sorry," Gracie lied. "I'm *so* close to making this combo work. I've run the numbers a billion times. It just has some weird timing."

"Okay." Alan didn't sound quite convinced, but he didn't argue with her either. He laid down a mass heal-over-time spell and switched briefly to the party channel. "Everyone in the glowing circle, thank you." To Gracie, he said, "Kind of hard on Caspian, though."

"Eh, the kid seems up to it." Caspian was doing remarkably well, Gracie had to say. His time playing *WoW* must have stood him in very good stead. "Anyway, what better time to break him in? Nice low-stakes…"

"Right." Alan gave a little laugh. "So this is how we haze people now, huh? Run a terrible dungeon and let them think they just failed to hold it together?"

"It's a legit form of trolling, and I won't hear another word against it." Gracie laughed. "Okay, we're all healed. Hang in there, buddy."

She didn't wait for Alan to respond. She walked to place the gem, the relic of the demon's body, in a depression on the edge of the island. The stones that formed the next path rose soundlessly out of the dark water and Gracie started across them.

This time, because she was looking for it, she saw the faint movement in the darkness: the lake monster, the one she had fought before. Her heart quickened. She could let the monster kill her, couldn't she? Yes. It had killed Ushanas rather spectacularly last time.

More islands lay in their way, and Gracie began to find patterns she could use to just barely keep the fights going. She could hear the rest of the DPS panting, and the magic users were running on empty by the time they came to the main island.

They had to be, of course. Gracie kept them going, knowing that each minute she dragged the fights out was one less minute they had to regain health and mana. One less chance they would have to save the final boss fight as she took it in the wrong direction. This team was good. She didn't want anyone pulling a Hail Mary at the last moment.

"We should rest up," Alan said quietly.

"No time." Gracie took off, running for the line of fire that would close off the portal. There was silence, but people fell in behind her. She thought she saw Jay and Alan exchange looks out of the corner of her eye. She wondered what they were thinking.

Maybe that all of her success had been luck, and she'd lost whatever spark of inspiration was keeping her going?

The thought rankled more than it should have. She wanted to tell them that she was messing up on purpose. That was just leftover pride from her childhood, though, she figured. She'd never been the golden child, and she'd spent years trying to gain her parents' respect.

And then years doing exactly what they *didn't* want her to do.

"Real mature, Gracie," she muttered to herself.

When the eel slithered out of the lake, she felt a wave of satisfaction, quickly drowned only by a wave of sadness. Sadness? She shook her head. She *wanted* to end this.

"Everyone stay back while I get threat!" she called. "I want to try out that combo again. Eighty-fifth time's the charm!"

She'd die, and this would all be over.

But the lake monster didn't close the group in. Instead, it left a gap through which the giant returned. The whip of fire was curled loosely in one hand, and the kelp of his beard dripped on the ground.

The giant stared at her. It had not enclosed them in a bubble this time, and Gracie dropped her sword tip down, approaching him.

"It's you," she said quietly.

"Why did you come back?" Harry asked her. His character had no expression, but she could deduce from his voice that his eyes were narrowed.

"Why did you choose this zone?" Gracie asked him instead.

"Immortality makes a fetish of death."

"Miss me with that philosophical bullshit and speak plainly." Gracie brought her sword up again. "And fight me, goddammit."

In answer, Harry let the whip flick out.

"Gracie—" Jay's voice said in her ear.

Gracie shut down the channel without answering. She began to circle, her eyes fixed on Harry.

"Do you not see?" Harry asked her. "I'm disappointed."

"Yeah, well, neither of us exactly planned on me being your protege, did we? So maybe you got stuck with a dud." Gracie smiled humorlessly. She danced into range, attacked, and headed out a touch too slowly, feeling the haptics shudder and watching her life bar take a hit. "Close the rest of them out. Let's do this with just us."

Harry held up one hand, and the bubble came up to seal them in. Gracie could see the others circling.

"Dragon Soul is watching," he said.

"You noticed that, did you?" Gracie asked him. "So you have a big audience. You love that, don't you?" She wanted to piss him off, but it definitely helped that she meant all the words she was hurling at him. "Tell us what grand, *deep* reasons you had for putting part of the quest here?"

The whip lashed at her, and this time she was reminded that Harry had dreamed this world from nothing. He was *quick*. It was his territory.

"Deprived of mortality, the gods lost their reason to be," he said. "What exists in a world without death? What is there to *fear*? Nothing. And so they became monsters, trying to make an ally of the one thing they most feared, and the one thing they craved. In their weakness, they inflicted all manner of torture on others. They savored the screams, and dreamed themselves in the place of the offerings."

Dude, this is fucked up. Gracie wondered if any of the rest of them could hear the monologue.

"And what is a player in this world?" Harry asked. "A god. They cannot die, so they too descend to the level of beasts and monsters. I told you the truth, *Callista*. I fear what humans will become in a world where they may inflict pain without consequence."

"Then maybe you shouldn't have built that world," Gracie told him. She shook her head once, a hard jerk. "And maybe you shouldn't be wasting your time with Jay and me when you can apparently get into the game's framework just fine on your own."

"What?" She had thrown Harry off. He stopped, forgetting to attack.

Gracie landed a rather harder blow than she'd intended. She headed back out of range and watched.

"Who is Jay?" Harry asked.

Gracie narrowed her eyes, but she didn't drop her sword. "I don't know what you call him. The…" *Guy you're using to get into the game.* She bit the words off. If Dragon Soul was listening, she didn't want them to know what she was going to say.

"They can't hear us right now," Harry told her as if reading her mind.

"Why are you using Jay to get into the database if you're able to do things like this?" Gracie demanded. "What do you think *Jay* can do to unravel the quest if you can't?"

"I don't understand." Harry looked at her. "I've been trying to get you unhooked from the quest, yes, but I made that next to impossible. You have to die in one of the quest segments in order for that to happen." He snapped the whip at her again.

"So that's why you're here," Gracie said. "Well, let me tell you, you're welcome to it. Kill me. I don't want this. Just promise me you'll leave Jay out of it, and the rest of the guild, too."

"For the last time, I don't know who Jay is!"

And then it snapped into place. Gracie's jaw dropped. "Son of a bitch!"

"Let's get this over with." Harry lashed at her with the whip.

Gracie rolled to the side, just out of the way of the whip. "Stop for a second. Just stop!"

"You said you wanted me to kill you." Harry readied another strike.

"But don't you see?" Gracie demanded. "Jay hasn't been talking to you at all, has he? They've been using him to keep track of our progress. Dan and Dhruv are pretending to be you. He's been talking to *you*."

Harry laughed. "I'm surprised Dan had the balls for that, but he always was clever. It was just executing on his own plans that he was too scared to do."

"Yeah, well—" Gracie rolled out of the way of another strike. "Goddammit, stop for a second! I need to think."

"You'll have plenty of time to think," Harry said, "when this is over. Stand still. After all, this won't hurt a bit."

But now, in this split second, anger blazed to life in her chest and Gracie found the will to stay in the game. She didn't want Harry to have the power, and right now, she was more than willing to be the queen bitch that was a thorn in the side of Dragon Soul.

They'd been fucking with her for weeks, and she was going to make them pay.

CHAPTER SIXTEEN

Something had been off since the beginning of the run. Jay had noticed Gracie's nervous mannerisms and her overall reticence, and above all, her failure to pull off the feats she usually accomplished with ease. It wasn't like her to fail, and it was even *more* unlike her to fail repeatedly when other people were involved.

It was almost like she wanted the dungeon to fail, he reflected.

Or maybe it was *exactly* like she wanted the dungeon to fail. He realized that in the moment that she went charging into the final boss fight, not waiting for cooldowns. She'd set it up so that there wasn't time for them to wait, and there wasn't time for anyone to pull out a last-second save. She hadn't messed up and hamstrung them by accident, she'd done it a hundred percent on purpose so they couldn't help her.

What she was trying to do, Jay couldn't guess. He knew there were things she hadn't told him about her conversation with Harry. When she came back, she'd been sober, reserved, and almost guilty. No matter how Jay pushed, knowing that he knew more of the backstory than she did, he hadn't been able to convince her that she should share it.

Beyond anything, he was afraid that she was giving up. That she was giving the quest back to Harry.

Harry didn't deserve it. Jay wanted to scream. Gracie might not want the role she'd been given. She might not think she was the best one for it, but he would rather have her in power than *any* of the founders of Dragon Soul.

But it was her choice, and he took a deep breath and made his own.

He would help her. Whatever she was doing, he would help her.

He watched as the giant climbed out of the lake and approached. The snake wasn't attacking them yet, although he could see its head swaying in the darkness. Gracie and the giant spoke, their words not quite audible.

"Uh, Anders?" Lakhesis sounded unsure. "You want me going for that tail?"

"Is this what happened last time?" Jay heard Caspian ask. Alan silently shook his head.

"Everyone wait," Jay said. He fought the urge to explain. "Wait for my signal. This may not be a battle, but I want Team 2 ready to go for the tail at my mark, okay?"

There was a chorus of assent. Team 2 was Lakhesis, Chowder, Ushanas, Caspian, and Dathok. All of them readied themselves, and although several of them looked at Jay, none seemed ready to force the issue of what, exactly, was going on.

That was good, since he didn't have a clue what to say.

He watched, his chest tightening, as Gracie rolled out of the way of the strikes and the bubble came up. She was moving more slowly than she could, taking damage she could easily have avoided.

And then the tenor of it changed. He could see her posture take on the tension of a fight, hear her yelling, even if he couldn't make out the words. She was trying to stop the fight from progressing now, but he couldn't imagine why.

The monster didn't intend to let that happen. He went on the offensive, fiery whip lashing toward Gracie as she tried desperately to avoid it.

"*Gracie!*" He barely heard himself yell her name. He was running for the bubble, trying to get to her, but there was no way to get through. Inside the bubble, he heard her yell something, and the lash slammed against the edge of the enclosure, right over Jay's face. He jerked back.

And then he heard yelling. The lake monster had closed itself into a tight circle and was preparing to attack.

"Team 2!" Lakhesis yelled. "Go! I'll go for the head. It can fight back, so that's where a tank is needed. Jay, come on!"

Jay gave one last look at Gracie and ran to help the rest of the team. There was no time to think about what was going on with her. All they could do was hold up their end and hope it was enough.

It was Jamie's first dungeon run with Red Squadron, and frankly, he wasn't impressed with what he was seeing of

Callista. He'd watched the video of her month-first run, and she'd been better there. Maybe it had been a fluke.

He'd been so caught up with his smug sense of annoyance that it had taken him longer than it should to notice the looks people were giving one another. This was unusual, and after the second boss fight, Alan had opened a private channel.

"Hey," Alan had said awkwardly. "Uh…look, just hang in there, okay?"

"What's going on?" Jamie asked him. Alan clearly wanted to say more, and Jamie wished the other man weren't so loyal to Callista. *Go on,* he thought, *admit she's not all you thought she was.*

Alan hesitated. "I've never seen her like this," he said finally. "It's like she's trying to screw up, but I can't figure out why she'd do that. Look, I know it's hellish to try to manage on one of your first dungeon runs, but hang in there. Trust me, *no one* is going to give you grief if we wipe. You're doing a great job."

"Right." Jamie fought a twist of guilt. Even now, people were trying to be nice to him. Trying to reassure him.

When Alan first said that Callista was trying to screw up, Jamie had thought the man was grasping at straws, but the more he watched, the more it seemed like Alan was correct. The occasional slip-up, Jamie could understand. Everyone missed things. But Callista went unerringly in the wrong direction, keeping things in a tightly-controlled band of not-quite-good-enough that wasn't erratic so much as remarkably consistent.

When the giant appeared out of the lake, and the lake monster, the group had murmured. They didn't seem particularly surprised at the start. Jamie looked around in awe. He'd run the Altar of the Gods several times, and he'd thought about how terrifying it would be if something came out of the black water.

Now it had. The lake beast was huge and had glistening scales, and in the darkness high above, Jamie caught glints of something that might be eyes or might be teeth, and he felt the terrifying sense of being prey.

The giant was no less amazing, something both dead and alive, cursed and powerful.

And then everything went tits over taint, as one of Jamie's guildmates liked to say, and he forgot anything except surviving.

"Team 2, go for the tail!" Lakhesis called.

"Cas!" Anders was charging into battle and didn't take the time to open a private channel. "When we say run, you get out through the opening between the tail and the body. *Run*, do you understand?"

"Got it!" Jamie called back. He noticed that the body was swaying, and strange AoE damage he couldn't understand was beginning to hit members of the group. "Mirra, I'm laying down my group heal!"

"Thanks!" Alan called back. "Stand by Chowder. He'll buff you."

Jamie moved into position gratefully, watching his health dip down in chunks, matched only barely by the heal he'd laid down.

Come on, come on, come on, come on... He shot heals at Chowder, Dathok, Ushanas, and himself—and then another, desperately, at Alan, who was trying to keep up with a larger group and was clearly thrown off by the damage coming out of nowhere.

"Thanks!" Alan called again.

"We're almost through the tail," Chowder yelled at the group. "Get ready to run!"

The ground was shuddering and rocking, Jamie's haptics buzzing almost constantly, and he found himself dizzy with it. The whole room was tipping—

"Run!" Anders yelled, and the whole group took off. Chunks of stone and ribbons of fire were falling from the ceiling, and Jamie could hardly see anything. He barely managed to follow the white of Alan's robes and gave a yell when the tail tightened behind him.

"Holy shit." His heart was pounding.

"No time to watch," Alan yelled. "*Heal!*"

Jamie fumbled opened his inventory and drank down a potion. With his mana shooting up, he could lay down more heals, all of the group clustered together and drinking potions, trading food in whatever sliver of time they had. From the panicked calls, Jamie knew this was nothing like what had happened last time.

He wanted to laugh. He couldn't help it. This was exhilarating. He normally went into dungeons after watching extensive tutorials and training on formations. Everyone knew exactly what was going to happen and what their role was, and there was hell to pay if they didn't follow through.

Right now, he had zero idea what was going to happen, and it was the most fun he'd ever had in *Metamorphosis*. He didn't know if they were going to make it, but they were trying, and they were watching out for each other. He'd managed to keep Alan from dying back there, and he'd heard a dozen other exchanges where different players had helped one another.

There was a faint murmur of surprise, and he turned. Even Alan had stopped healing, watching what was going on inside the sphere.

Fire was roaring, the light so bright that it cast shadows into relief on the sides of the bubble: Callista, her golden armor shining like a beacon, and the giant with his whip. They were locked in battle, never stopping. Never even pausing, and Jamie wondered if they'd so much as noticed the flames all around them.

The head of the snake could be seen dipping toward the bubble, but even it could not get inside. With a shriek, it relaxed its body to let them back into the circle.

"Come on!" Jamie yelled. He led the charge back inside, running next to Anders, and he gave a whoop of joy as the DPS launched into their attacks once more.

He had no idea what was coming next, and he *loved* it.

"What the *hell* is going on?" Thad demanded. He looked at the conference call speaker for a moment before turning his attention back to the fight unfolding on the screen. "I've run Altar of the Gods at *least* a dozen times, and I have never *once* seen that. What the hell?"

"It's..." one of the founders of Dragon Soul began before letting his voice trail off.

"A glitch, huh?" Thad asked. "Hell of a glitch, isn't it?

That's not an NPC she's fighting, and it's not a boss. That's a player, isn't it?"

There was no answer, and Thad blew out his breath. He watched as Jamie threw out heals desperately, trying to keep the group alive. They were heading for a wipe, that much was unmistakable, but they were trying. Through all of the insanity, they were trying.

Thad crossed his arms, narrowed his eyes, and waited. Inside the bubble, Callista was fighting, and although they could hear everything happening on the party chat, they couldn't hear her.

The truth came to him a moment later: neither could Dragon Soul. They hadn't fixed this because they didn't know what was going on. The person Callista was fighting *wasn't* one of them.

So who was it?

"The quest is *mine!*" Harry yelled over the roar of the flames. The sound was so realistic, the heat wavering in the air, that Gracie could practically feel the flames licking at her cheek.

Gracie heard a crack and a crash from behind her and rushed him. She'd begun to see the patterns in how he moved, the speed with which he brought the whip down. When he thought he had her in his sights, he would lash to one side, driving her away, and lash again, and then lash much more quickly directly at her.

This time she was ready. With her health bar at half, she zigged left in response to his first lash, then zagged hard right, edging under the second strike and skidding towards him.

A whip wasn't good in close quarters, and that gave her a precious few seconds. Grace spun and flung her arm out, slamming the edge of her shield into the giant's legs. In terms of the game mechanics, a hit was a hit, but she was picturing how much it would hurt to take a shield to the kneecaps.

Hopefully, Harry was too.

"Give it up!" Harry yelled. "This isn't yours; it came to you by mistake! It was supposed to be *me!*"

"Well, try not being an asshole next time!" Gracie screamed back. She circled away and gave a hiss of annoyance as she stepped into the fire. She couldn't afford to be taking damage like that, not when she was cut off from her healers. They, she noticed, were currently dealing with what looked like total chaos outside. "And leave my team the fuck alone!"

"You shouldn't have brought them here," Harry said furiously. "This was between *us*. You knew what you had to do, and now you're going back on it so you can keep something that isn't yours." The whip lashed out.

Gracie barely got the shield up in time, crouching to activate one of her protection buffs. Her arms and legs were screaming at her, but she couldn't stop, not for a moment. She didn't bother answering him.

She'd felt bad for all of them for a while—him, Dragon Soul, and the other guilds. They hadn't asked for this, after all.

On the other hand, they'd repeatedly made the choice to go about all of this in literally the most fucked up way she could think of. They were messing with an entire group of people because they weren't creative enough to think of a better way, and didn't have enough balls to own up to the fact that it was a problem.

And like *hell* was she going to let them all get away with it. She knew just what would happen if she let Harry take the quest over: the founders would tear Dragon Soul apart and destroy the world she loved so much.

Fuck that.

Gracie fired off one of the combos she'd been keeping in reserve, activating her buffs as she kicked, shield-slammed, and slashed with all her might. She was close. She was so damned close to pulling this off.

"Why won't you *die?*" Harry yelled at her.

She didn't waste her breath replying. She was in her own world, feeling the breath burning in her throat and her muscles working beyond the limits of what she'd thought they could do. She wasn't going to just back down because they wanted her to. She wasn't going to give this up anymore.

Because now she had something to fight for.

She whirled and leapt over a patch of fire, crouched, and scanned the area quickly. An idea was forming in her head.

She was in range of Harry, laying down the groundwork before she danced sideways just in time to evade a crack of his whip. She gave a parting shot and whooped when it came up as a lucky crit. *Take that, motherfucker.*

He was angry now, and angry people made mistakes. Gracie felt her smile spreading cold across her face as she lured him onward, pivoting him just slightly each time she engaged. She'd nearly fallen head-first into a vat of flames —a giant crack in the floor—and now it was just behind her.

She just had to time this right. She turned and sprinted, pushing her character as hard as she could go and leaping at the last second. She was so engaged that she actually *did* jump, and stumbled into the red wall of the VR area.

But she'd done it. A yell of fury behind her made her turn, and she saw Harry's health bar dipping, dipping…

He climbed out, the kelp of his beard still incongruously dripping, and she knew he was past seeing how low his health was.

She wasn't, though. He charged her and Gracie stood her ground. She could take a hit, even a critical hit if she needed to, and he couldn't. She waited until the last second and then she dropped, slamming her fist into the ground for a blast wave and hearing his scream of frustration as his character died.

There was a moment of silence. The bubble disappeared and the flames died, and Gracie was standing in the middle of a scorched plain, staring at the others.

They couldn't hug, not really, but Jay was at her side in a moment, his arms wrapped through her body. They both laughed as their attempt to hug left them holding empty air.

"What the *hell* was that?" Jay demanded, breaking the moment. On purpose, Gracie suspected.

She stepped back and gave a laugh. "I was going to give up the quest. Let them fight it out."

"But?" Jay crossed his arms.

"But I don't trust any of them to be a god," Gracie said

simply. "They'd tear *Metamorphosis* apart. Oh, and one other thing…the person you've been talking to? It's not Harry."

"Son of a…" Jay's character had his usual, serene expression, but she could just picture his frown in real life. "Oh, God, and now they have records that I went into the database—"

"We'll deal with that," Gracie said. "in the meantime, let's get out of here. I don't trust Harry not to come back." She exchanged nods with Jay and waved at the rest of the group with her sword. "Let's GTFO, guys. And Cas, good job with everything we threw at you today. Hope it wasn't too much of a clusterfuck."

"No." Caspian's voice was amused, but he also sounded almost pensive. "I, uh…I actually had a pretty good time. It was fun."

There was a round of guffaws.

"Our kind of guy," Chowder said, clapping Caspian on the back. "Let's buy this dude a beer, huh?"

Gracie smiled as she teleported back, the world dissolving around her. She felt an ease she hadn't felt in a long time. She still might not have any idea where this quest was going, but she was damned if she was going to let any of the Dragon Soul founders destroy what they'd built just to act out old grudges.

CHAPTER SEVENTEEN

Red Squadron swept into one of Kithara's smaller taverns on a high. The few other playing characters who were there pivoted to look as the group ran in, jumping on tables and doing victory dances. Kevin managed to get his character's amarok up on one of the tables as well, and it wasn't long before people started dancing in a circle around it.

Gracie laughed and headed to the bar. It was funny to see the bartender waiting patiently, completely unaware of the chaos going on around him. In a real bar, she reflected, they would have been kicked out by now.

"Holy crap," a player said. They had been selling excess inventory to one of the vendors in the corner, and now they came over. "You're *Callista*."

"You think the nameplate gave it away?" Jay asked privately.

Gracie stifled a laugh. "Hi," she said awkwardly. "Sorry for the chaos. We just did a dungeon run, and everyone's kind of keyed up."

"No, that's cool. I just wanted to say hi!" The character waited awkwardly. "Uh, anyway. I'll go. Wait! Can I get a screenshot with you?"

"Er…okay." Gracie stood next to her, trying to decide whether or not to pose, but a second later, the player said, "Thanks!" and ran out of the tavern.

"Awww," Jay said. "Baby's first celebrity encounter. I think you can assume that's going to happen a lot."

Gracie sighed. She ordered two trays of beers and picked a mug up. "I wish these were real."

"You have any beer at home?" Jay asked her.

"Yeah, I think so."

"So, have a fake round here, let them all toast you, and then log off, and we'll have a beer over Skype."

"Sounds good." Gracie emoted a smile at him. "All right, Fys, get that wolf off the table. What, were you born in a barn? Everyone, beers are here."

Everyone gave a cheer and picked up one of the drinks. When Gracie lifted hers, they all followed suit.

"I know that was a weird, weird run of Altar of the Gods," Gracie said, "but we fucking *rocked* it. Big shout-out to Cas, who did his first dungeon run healing, and who I think we can all agree was a rock star. Cas, man, you're a natural!"

There was a round of cheers. Caspian raised his beer, apparently shy enough that he didn't have any words.

"Another big shout-out to Alan, who trained Cas."

People cheered again and clinked mugs.

"Shout-out to Dathok for trying some DPS, and for all the rest of you for making a plan and adapting on the fly when everything went sideways. Lakhesis and Jay, I understand I have you to thank for getting everyone into the right places?"

Lakhesis and Jay raised their mugs.

"I am so glad I met all of you," Gracie said sincerely. "I can't think of a better group to discover this crazy game with."

This time there was a louder round of cheers, so deafening that Gracie hunched her shoulders, laughing while her headset vibrated with the sound.

"I love you all," she said after she had finished her pixelated beer, "but my legs want to kill me right now, so I'm going to go collapse on the couch. Have a good night, everyone."

"Bye, Gracie!" people called.

"Bye, Callista," she heard Caspian murmur. She emoted a smile at him before she logged out. After the fire and whip-lashing insanity of the Altar of Gods, it was jarring for Gracie to take off her VR helmet and find an empty, dark apartment. Of course, she thought. Alex was off with Sydney. She wished he'd been there to see that dungeon run, but she'd tell him about it later.

She had just grabbed a beer and a bag of chips when her computer started ringing. She hobbled over, whimpering in protest as her leg muscles screamed.

"I'm trying to get there. I'm trying. Oh God, it hurts. Ow. I'm coming, I swear, I promise." She leaned over to hit the button and fell sideways onto the couch, holding the beer up to keep it from spilling.

Jay laughed. "You've turned into a disembodied hand and a bottle of beer."

"Mmf. Can't...sit...up." Gracie considered the beer. "Which makes drinking this difficult."

"Into every life comes some struggle," Jay said solemnly. "Be strong, fearless leader."

Gracie forced herself to sit up and took a sip. "Oh, beer, what I wouldn't do for you."

"I'm sure it loves you too." Jay shook his head. "Now, because I am losing my mind just a little bit, what the *fuck* is going on with Harry? And Dan and Dhruv."

"Right." Gracie settled back. "Soooo, let's start with Dan and Dhruv. Long story short, Harry says he hasn't been emailing you, and I believe him. I think Dragon Soul was using you to try to find the quest."

"It makes so much sense." Jay sounded furious. "All those emails where they'd suggest that things *might* be in a certain zone, but they wouldn't tell me what they'd supposedly left there? That big email he sent that was a whole bunch of nothing. They wanted me to go hunting for things, just like they had when I was working there."

"Dangerous game, though," Gracie pointed out, "because I got that armor out of it, and I don't know if you noticed, but my crit chance has gone *way* up."

"Which must have made it especially difficult to suck so much on that run," Jay said pointedly.

"Yeahhhh." Gracie looked down at her lap and tried to think of what to say. "Okay, don't be mad."

"I'm not mad, Gracie." His voice was quiet. "I just wish I'd known. I would have helped you. Any of us would have." He considered. "And, uh, what did Harry do to make you go all medieval on his ass?" There was a laugh bubbling up in his voice now.

"It wasn't so much him… Well, it was kind of him. It was when I figured out that Dragon Soul was really the one emailing you. He was trying to fight it out with them, and they were trying to mess with us. It was just too *stupid*, you know? They made this beautiful world, and now they're trying to rip it apart with sponsorships and old grudges and…"

Jay waited.

Gracie looked at the far wall and considered. In the dark quiet of the apartment, the world of *Metamorphosis* seemed far more vivid than anything here. If she closed her eyes, she could see flames dancing on the ground and the fiery whip coming towards her—

"If I gave the quest back to Harry," Gracie explained, "he'd have tried to control all the players, and go to war with Dan and Dhruv. If I gave it up and he *didn't* get it, they'd keep undermining the world with their sponsorships and backstabbing. I guess I wanted to keep them in line." She gave a self-conscious laugh. "Which is ridiculous. But I actually fucking care about this place. That team."

"You get to," Jay said. "And I think at this point, you get to ask some hard fucking questions of them as well. They should be living in fear of you coming to them to ask them what the hell they think they're playing at." He considered. "At the risk of you repeating yourself, what even *happened* in there? I'm guessing that if you had lost that fight, Harry would have gotten the quest back."

"Yeah," Gracie said. "He built it so it was almost impossible to take out. I don't know what that even means."

"Neither do I, honestly." Jay frowned. "I'll have to go back over the bits of the quest that I found and see how they're embedded. It shouldn't be very difficult to just take the lines of code out, but lord knows what else he put in there. Anyway, go on."

"So, since he couldn't take the quest out, the only way for him to get it back for himself was for me to fail at it," Gracie explained. "See?"

"So you took us back to Altar of the Gods, hoping we'd get the same boss—which was actually Harry, right?—and we'd wipe and you'd be done with all of that craziness."

"Bingo." Gracie held up her beer in a toast before taking a sip. "God, I'm ravenous. Anyway, by the time I realized I wanted to keep the quest, I was already down to half a life, and he was pulling out all the stops. Oh, well."

Jay began to laugh. "Just imagine how much that's pissing him off." He rotated his shoulders and stood. "Ugh, I need to stretch. I can *feel* my muscles cramping." He disappeared out of the frame. "The more we play, the more I feel like *Metamorphosis* is a government conspiracy to get more people in shape for the Army or something."

"Trick the nerds into doing exercise," Gracie said thoughtfully. "It's a good idea. Otherwise, I would come home, tell myself I *should* work out, and then not work out." She put her beer on the coffee table and stood, reaching down to touch her toes. The backs of her legs cramped, her back screamed, and she winced as things gradually began to loosen. "Oh, this is hellish."

"Uh-huh." Jay gave an anguished noise, and there was a crash. "It's fine, I'm fine, everything's fine here. How are you?"

Gracie fought to hold in her laughter. Her abs hurt.

Moving hurt. "Lesson learned: never fight an angry giant with a whip made of fire."

"Valid," Jay said contemplatively. He appeared briefly in the frame as he righted himself. "So, here's where I'm at… Harry clearly has *some* access to the database, but made the quest complex enough that it's difficult to alter."

"He probably didn't just take it *out* because he wanted to pick it up when I failed," Gracie said. "So that was why we had those fights where it felt like I was fighting a real person. I was. He was trying to get me to fail." She looked up in time to see Jay take a seat, clearly pondering. "So the first question is, will he keep trying to make me fail the quest or will he just take it out?"

"Hard to know," Jay replied after a moment. "You've put him in a bit of a bind. The farther you get, the more he can assume Dragon Soul knows about what's going on. They can do the research I could and try to remove the quest. On the other hand, it doesn't sound like he has a better way to stop you from completing it."

Gracie sighed. "He's batshit loonball, isn't he?"

"They all are, as far as I'm concerned." Jay considered. "There's also the part where they're almost certainly spying on us. I don't know if your account is tagged or what. It probably is. And they may have tried to embed someone."

"Who?" Gracie asked reasonably. "Everyone who was there tonight signed on a while back. Well, except Cas." Her voice trailed off. "Oh, son of a *bitch*. Cas."

"Who's so very, very quick to pick up healing," Jay said. "Well, I'll be damned."

"You think he works for Dragon Soul?" Gracie narrowed her eyes.

"I'll ask Sam," Jay replied after a moment. "He'll be able to find out. It wouldn't be anyone on my old team, that's for sure, and they'd have had to keep it quiet or someone *on* my old team would have told me." He sighed. "Let's not jump to conclusions, though. It might not be him."

"It is," Gracie said with certainty. Little things she hadn't noticed, little silences and stray words, Caspian's reticence. It was all fitting together now.

There was a long silence.

"What do you want to do?" Jay asked her finally.

"I want to finish the quest," Gracie said. "I want to figure out where the rest of it is, and finish it. The question is…"

"How do we do that without one or the other of those groups stopping us?" Jay finished. He sighed. "Let's get some sleep, and tomorrow we'll figure it out."

Gracie nodded. "Thanks for being there tonight," she said. She smiled at him. "I'm sorry I didn't tell you what I was trying to do."

"I get it." Jay gave a small smile back. "Crazy god-queen or not, you're *our* tank, and we're keeping you around. You can't get rid of us that easily."

Gracie laughed and ended the call. She sighed as she brushed her teeth and washed her face, wishing she had Alex around to share another beer with—and ask about Jay. She left the hall light on and went to bed, where she flopped back and stared into the darkness.

Part of her hated all these games.

And part of her wanted more than anything to win them.

CHAPTER EIGHTEEN

Sam pulled off the highway, drumming his hands nervously on the steering wheel. He'd been home last night when Callista's team made their run, and one of his team members had kept him updated on it by text. No one seemed to be sure what exactly had happened, but they seemed sure that it *wasn't* the same as what had happened the first time her group had gone through the Altar of the Gods.

When Sam had asked what that meant, he'd been told it was too much to say over text, but that Dan and Dhruv had stayed late afterward, arguing in Dhruv's office.

Sam really didn't want to go to work today. He wanted to go home, drink some coffee, and take his daughter out of school for the day to go to the zoo or something. Normal stuff. Not one thing in his life seemed normal lately, and he was tired of it.

Which was why, when he pulled into his parking spot at the far edge of the lot and saw Jay waiting for him, leaning against his car, he swore inventively. He slammed the door as he got out of the car, jabbing his finger at Jay.

"No. *No.* No more of this shit. It's complicated enough as it is, and for the love of God, *don't* go into the database again, I have to tell them when you do, and I don't want to."

Jay stared at him for a moment quizzically. Then he opened his car door, reached inside, and brought out a breakfast sandwich and a coffee.

"Bribery?" Sam raised an eyebrow. "Really?" But his stomach betrayed him by growling. He sighed, grabbed the coffee and breakfast sandwich, and leaned against his own car to eat. "Why are you here? And what the hell happened last night at the Altar of the Gods?"

"It would kind of help if I knew exactly how much your dude overheard," Jay told him.

"They were watching the whole time," Sam said around a mouthful of egg and sausage. "Whole team. Not a dude."

"Really? You're just going to pretend you didn't embed someone in the guild?" Jay raised an eyebrow right back.

"Oh." Sam nodded. "The healer."

"*Yes.* Goddammit, Sam, you could have given me a heads up!" Jay ran a hand through his hair.

"First of all, I wasn't in last night, so I didn't know who was on that run. Second of all..." Sam sighed. "It's not our guy. He's from Demon Syndicate. We just have a feed in when he's playing."

"Oh, really?" Jay tipped his head back. "She's gonna hate this," he said to himself. "*Not* that you're to tell them that."

"Believe me, I'm trying to stay as far out of it as I can." Sam gave him a look. "I have a kid, man, I need this job. I don't like what they're doing, but I need this job." He hesitated. "And I gotta be honest, if you want to go up against the people who *run the damned servers,* you're gonna lose."

There was a long silence. Jay opened his car door again and slumped sideways into the driver's seat.

"Harry showed up at Gracie's apartment," he told Sam.

Sam stopped dead. "He *what?*"

"Yeah. Found out who she was, found out where she lived, and showed up to talk to her. Apparently, she broke his nose." Jay's shoulders shook with silent laughter.

"If ever someone deserved it," Sam said, "he's the guy."

"Yeah. Sam, if I tell you what's going on, will you either help *us* or keep it under your hat?"

"I don't like being in the middle," Sam said. "I don't like keeping secrets. I don't like doing shady shit."

"*Then help us,*" Jay said fiercely. "Sam, Harry's a nutjob. He's trying to screw everyone over, and Dan and Dhruv wound themselves into a clusterfuck by promising the sponsored guilds that they'd be on top of the rankings. If Gracie keeps going, she has leverage—and I'd much rather *she* have it than Harry or no one."

Sam chewed contemplatively. "Fine."

"Harry thought he'd be doing the quest," Jay said bluntly. "He's going to try to make Gracie fail it so that he can pick it up...or he'll try to nuke it all. Meanwhile, Dan and Dhruv have been fucking *catfishing* me."

"Yeah, I know." Sam sighed. "Well, I know they left your database access open to see what you'd do and where you'd look. The catfishing seems like it would go with that. Look, Jay, I don't know how I can help you—"

"Find out which levels Harry built," Jay said. "As subtly as you can since I don't want Dan and Dhruv knowing.

And anytime you can, just keep telling them to try to make Gracie an ally. Keep telling them to play it straight. Her winning is a rags-to-riches story they could milk for *thousands* of sign-ups if they were smart about it. They don't *need* to run this game on money from advertisers. Tell them to stop playing stupid games and just make this what it was supposed to be: a world for the players."

"All right, all right," Sam grumbled. "Enough with the soapbox. I get it." He heaved another sigh.

"They're making money hand over fist," Jay said, "and they *know* nothing's going to kill the game faster than people knowing it's pay-to-play. They're just trying to play both sides as long as they can."

"I know." Sam wished he didn't. He wished he could say this was all a revelation instead of something he'd been lying awake, thinking anxiously about as he failed to get to sleep at nights.

"Harry may have been a total asshole," Jay said, "but he got one thing right. Having leverage over the other two is a good idea. Sam, you say you need to keep this job, but what's going to happen if the Ds run this company into the ground?" He crossed his arms and gave Sam a knowing look.

"You've made your point." Sam finished his coffee. "I'll get you the list today, and I'll take whatever openings I have to tell them to be more ethical about things. Not sure how much they'll go for it, of course."

"You do what you can," Jay said with a shrug. "If I thought they'd listen to reason, I'd have a meeting with them myself. Or not be worrying about Gracie keeping the quest. It's worth a shot, right? Best case scenario, we have a big stick and don't have to use it."

"What do you think you're going to *do*?" Sam burst out. "Say I help you. Say she finishes this quest. What can she *possibly* do that would keep them accountable?"

"I'm not sure," Jay said, but he was smiling. "All I know is, Harry wouldn't have gone to this much trouble if it were *nothing*, right?"

Sam slung his work bag over his shoulder as he considered this and nodded finally. "That makes sense, I guess. Well, be smart. They can see almost everything you do, and they can *definitely* see when you go into the database. Well, I can. And since you're not supposed to be there, I can't justify not telling them."

Jay only smiled again. "We'll cross that bridge next," he said, and there was a certain sense of amusement in his voice.

"If you think you're going to make me a double agent—"

"Sam, you hate people playing dirty, and you know the Ds are being dumb. You're absolutely going to help because you want all your employees to keep having jobs. I know you." Jay grinned at him. "Have a good day at work."

Sam grumbled. He watched as Jay drove away, then he shook his head and headed into the building.

Jay was right. Sam had been dubious when he came on board. He wasn't really a gamer, so he'd taken the job more for the benefits than anything else. He hadn't expected to care so much about his team or get so invested in a world that didn't *quite* exist.

Because as much as people liked to make a distinction

between games and "real life," Sam was beginning to think those two weren't necessarily different things.

By the time Jay called, Gracie had made a list of dungeons in *Metamorphosis*, cross-referenced by any aspect she could think of, and she was beginning to feel like she was going insane.

"Hi," she said, looking up. She picked up the laptop and pivoted it so he could see the diagrams. "I've been working on things, and I have a list of dungeons I think are likely. My *big* question is how Harry knows when we go into them."

"Oh, shit." From his tone, Jay clearly hadn't thought of that. "I, uh…hmm…"

"How was Sam?" Gracie asked.

"Not very happy to be involved," Jay admitted. When she looked at him with a sympathetic grimace, he shrugged. "It's a weird place to be, right? We all love *Metamorphosis* and it wouldn't exist without those three, but they're all being insane about it."

Gracie nodded and sat back on the couch, thinking.

"Which levels are you thinking about?" Jay asked her.

"I have two main contenders." Gracie held up the sheets of paper. "Yesuan's Haunt, and Klauria Castle."

"I worked on Klauria a bit," Jay said, "but I know next to nothing about Yesuan's Haunt. I thought it wasn't part of the main storyline."

"It's not," Gracie confirmed. "There are four optional

dungeons, one for each of the playable races. They kind of go into what happened after the races got scattered."

Jay nodded.

Gracie paused. "Do you think Harry thinks of himself as an Aosi?" she asked slowly. "Like, he thinks he's better than everyone else, smarter than everyone else, and *meant* to lead?"

Jay groaned. "Oh, dear God, he probably does. This guy has the biggest chip on his shoulder!"

Gracie nodded. She was still thinking, and finally, she sighed. "At least he hasn't been back."

"Are you worried?" Jay leaned forward.

"A bit," Gracie admitted. "His whole thing is that he's worried about people doing the same stuff in real life that they do in the game, right? Well, in the game, we're in a battle to the death, so I really hope that when push comes to shove, he doesn't believe all that crap he's spewing."

"He doesn't," Jay assured her. He settled back in his chair. "Tell me about Yesuan's Haunt."

Gracie pulled the sheet of paper out and studied it. "The boss is a druid, except it's a corruption-type thing, so the mechanics are very focused on—"

"I meant the lore."

"Oh!" She lit up and bounced in her seat. "It's *really* cool. So, the Aosi were made to rule all the other races and be these benevolent dictator guys, right? Blah, blah, blah, boring…until it didn't work out, and now it's fun." She grinned. "In the canon, the Aosi actually have this *huge* reckoning and split into a few different groups because they're trying to grapple with the fact that they didn't do what they were supposed to do. So there are the ones who think the gods totally fucked up and the Aosi are just another mortal race, there are the ones who think it's *still* their destiny to go back and rule over everyone, and then there are all these other little groups. Some people went a bit crazy and super-religious, I think? Because the Aosi came down to earth with this mandate, and the gods scattered them and haven't talked to them again, so it's a whole big thing."

Jay was twirling a pen in his fingers, considering.

"*Yesuan*," Gracie said, "didn't join any of the factions, even though they all wanted him to. He was this big healer-dude who was important in the wars, and all of the factions thought if he joined, they'd 'win' and be able to pick a unified strategy as a group, right? Well, he kinda went off the deep end instead. He became convinced that the only way to balance things was to be the opposite of what the Aosi had been. Instead of leaders, they should step away from any sort of politics, and instead of life and peace, they should cultivate corruption and war. He believed that the Aosi would be a unifying force, but *only* if they became the force that the rest of the world unified *against*."

"Oh, *shit*." Jay had dropped the pen.

"So he started doing his thing, and trying to work his way back to the center of the world to find the other races," Gracie explained, "and the other Aosi magic wielders all came to the conclusion pretty quickly that this would be mega-bad, so they teamed up and imprisoned him on the assumption that eventually he would stop being bonkers and they could let him out."

"He didn't stop, did he?"

"Nah. When you go in there, he's still crazy as balls."

She grinned at him. "Now, it's worth noting that that's the lore of the dungeon as it stands. I have *no* idea what'll come up if it's one of Harry's dungeons, but it really does sound like him, doesn't it?"

"It really does," Jay agreed. He spun around in his chair as he considered. "Sam's checking which levels Harry worked on, and he should be getting that to me soon."

The door of the apartment opened, and Gracie frowned. She held a finger to her lips so Jay wouldn't say anything and reached stealthily for her phone.

"Gracie?" Alex called. "It's me."

"Oh, thank God." Gracie slumped back against the couch. "I thought you were Harry."

"Harry? What, did he come *here*?" Alex poked his head around the door. "I'm going to tear that motherfucker a new asshole."

Gracie looked him over. "Just as soon as you've showered and gotten some sleep, eh? You look like something the cat dragged in." She was snickering. "Go get cleaned up. I'll make some coffee."

"Thank you." Alex disappeared down the hallway.

Gracie looked back at the computer screen, grinning, and found Jay holding up his phone triumphantly.

"Yesuan's Haunt," he said, very satisfied. "Sam confirmed it: Harry *did* work on that one. He wrote all the lore, too."

"So now we just have to figure out how to get there without him knowing," Gracie said.

"And without Dan and Dhruv taking the servers down," Jay agreed.

"And we have to figure out what to do with Caspian," Gracie finished. "Ugh."

"Ugh, indeed. I say we go punch some bears and *then* figure it out."

"You're on." Gracie grinned at him. "Well, as soon as I get the coffee made. Alex looks *rough* but not devastated, so I'm assuming he just never got to sleep. We'll see." She winked and headed off to make a pot of coffee.

CHAPTER NINETEEN

This was how it should be, Jay thought. Just hanging out in-game, trying something fun for the hell of it. He and Gracie had switched their skill trees, both as Level 1 senders, and she was trying damage-dealing while he tried healing.

Neither of them was used to being squishy and without armor, though, and it showed. They kept barely escaping from fights in one piece, desperately fleeing in order to hide and drink as many health potions as they could.

"We suck at this," Gracie said bluntly after the fifth time that had happened.

Jay agreed with a groan. "Also, thank God for magical stretching robes that always fit, but I feel ridiculous in this getup."

"Now, now. Who says a man can't wear flowing sky-blue robes? Men's fashion is normally so *boring*." Gracie was laughing as she looked at him. "I think the beard really makes it."

Jay grumbled. "So, how's Alex?"

"Still in the shower. Possibly fell asleep there, but I'm not gonna check." Gracie held up her hands to absolve herself. "Rule one of roommates: *never* surprise them in the shower."

"Solid." Jay looked out over the field of gently-waving grass. "Okay, I see one fae on its own. Should we try to kill it?"

"I don't know. I can't seem to kill anything anymore." Gracie sounded grumpy. "Throw fireballs, they said. It'll be fun, they said. I want a *sword*. I want to punch things and kick them. None of this crazy fire-magic stuff."

"Come on, keep working at it." Jay was laughing. "Don't give up just yet. I believe in you."

"Ugh. You are one motivational quote away from getting throat-punched." Gracie shook a fist in his direction. "But I'll make you a deal. I kill that fae, and you figure out what to do with Caspian." She took off without looking back.

"Whoa! Hey, I did *not* agree to that!" Jay started running after her. "Come baaaaaaack. I don't want to make this decision. Maybe we just boot him and never talk to him again?"

"Ghost him?" Gracie called over her shoulder. "Isn't that rude?"

"I don't know. Infiltrating the group was pretty rude, right?"

"Well, you have me there." Gracie slammed into the fae at high speed with a punch. "Take that, bitch! OH. CRAP. I'm supposed to be throwing spells. RUUUUUUN!"

"Every time," Jay groaned, but he was laughing as they ran away. "I didn't think about it either. I just saw Callista running into combat, and I followed. It's what I do!"

"We *suck* at this." Gracie was holding her sides from her laughter. "God, we are *so bad* at it. No, don't stop! Don't try to heal, just run!"

"But I'm a healer!" Jay was yelling as their characters ran. Because the movements were automatically controlled, their characters' legs were acting as if they were running, while their arms made all the motions they would have in real life.

"You look like a lunatic, and you're about to be a dead lunatic!" Gracie called back. "Run! *Run!*"

They reached an outcropping and Gracie crouched, still laughing. Although she hadn't really been running, she was still out of breath from shouting and laughing and the mad adrenaline rush of their characters nearly dying.

"Okay," she said when she'd regained her breath. "Once more, but this time, not stupidly."

"Aye," Jay said.

They edged forward into battle again. Gracie tiptoed forward one step at a time until she was in range to cast spells. She had learned the range of all of her tanking abilities, but didn't yet know all of the ranges of her spell-casting abilities. She threw a fireball and waited for the fae to notice.

Not surprisingly, the fae seemed to object to being lit on fire. It turned around with a shriek and headed toward Gracie at high speed, and she tried to burn it down with fireballs before it reached her.

"Fuck! Ow! Get off! Go away!"

"You're trying to kill it," Jay called from a little way away as he healed her. "It probably isn't going to listen to you."

"Yes. I got that. Thank you." Gracie flailed her arms and muttered angrily as the fae interrupted her spell-casting. "Just one…more…freaking… Oh, fuck it." She launched a flurry of punches to finish off the fae.

"Not really committing to this spell-caster thing, are you?" Jay called to her.

"Listen, man, sometimes you just need to punch something until it dies." She picked up a few gold coins that had dropped, and the game automatically divided them between her inventory and Jay's. "I'm not sure I like spell-casting."

"I think you might like frost mage better," he suggested. "You control the board, and snare them and slow them down. They can't get to you easily to interrupt your spell-casting."

"Hell, yeah, I'd like that better." Gracie scouted for another lone fae. "This glass cannon thing is not for me."

"Well, a frost mage can be like a glass cannon. It's just like…I don't know, sniping in a first-person shooter. You *have* to set up the fight or you get dead pretty quickly." Jay trailed after her, a surprisingly serene hulking barbarian in sky-blue robes with pretty gold embroidery.

"Ugh. Gimme a sword and a shield any day." Gracie grinned at him. "You look *very* dashing in those robes, though, let me tell you."

Jay groaned. "Don't mention that, please. My pride is

taking a beating. In a totally enlightened, 21st century, modern sort of way, my masculinity cannot take this."

"Maybe it's making you stronger," Gracie suggested encouragingly. "You have to remain manly in a baby-blue dress, and now you'll be manly in anything."

"Did you have to describe it as a dress?" He sounded anguished.

Gracie just snickered. "Heads up, new target." She inched forward. "Okay, so what the hell do we do about Caspian?"

Jay sighed and touched off a corruption spell on their target. "I don't know," he said resignedly as the fae raced towards them, shrieking. "Do we try to get details out of *him*? Or do we tell him we know who he is and try to turn him into a double agent? We could go a few ways with this."

"We're not going to turn him into a double agent," Gracie said, trying to hold her focus and not resort to physical attacks. It took a peculiar kind of courage to keep spell-casting while an opponent beat you around the head and neck, it turned out.

Hell, with the haptics shuddering, it even *felt* real. No bruises, of course, and no real blood, but it was surprising how little it took to make your body believe it was in a fight.

They finished the fight, and she sighed as she looted the body. "I don't know. Do *you* think he'd ever work for us?"

Jay thought about this as they headed to the next fae encampment. "You know, what's weird is that I thought he really enjoyed the Altar of the Gods."

Gracie looked at him as they walked. It was difficult to

do in the game without wandering off-track...rather like walking in real life, she thought. "Yeah, what happened with all of you while I was fighting Harry, anyway?"

"Well, we were all waiting, and then the lake monster went crazy. He was clearly trying to make sure we couldn't help you, and all we could think was that we didn't want him to win. Lakhesis really stepped up, and Caspian just launched into action. I could hear him laughing—you know the way someone laughs when they're pulling off something they didn't think was possible? Like that. He'd give these happy yells when he got someone healed just in time, and he and Alan were shouting back and forth, trading targets. He was on a high after that. He really seemed into it."

Gracie said nothing. In a way, this pissed her off even more. That should be a memory *her* team had, she thought —a time when they'd bonded with each other, with people who supported them.

Instead, they'd had a double agent, which was—

"It's just fucking ridiculous," she said, biting off each word. "This isn't some high-stakes diplomatic crisis. It's not the goddamned hunt for Red October. *It's a video game, Jay.*"

"I know." Jay reached out to pat her shoulder. "Whoops. Keep forgetting you're not actually right there."

"They could have asked me to roll a new character," Gracie said, waving her hands.

"This one would still be sitting in the rankings. I mean, I know there were other ways to handle it, but all of the basic things? Yeah, they tried those. They tried deleting you. They tried banning you. They tried doing a server reset. Whatever the hell Harry did, you're in there good." Jay was laughing. "That son of a bitch played himself, and I love it."

Gracie grinned. "Okay, that part, I *do* like. One sec." She had felt footsteps nearby recently and wondered if Alex was going to come play. When she took off her VR helmet, though, she saw him passed out on the couch, snoring. "Okay, need to go get a blanket for Sleeping Beauty, here. Good Lord, can he snore!"

"Even I can hear that," Jay said. "That's impressive."

"At least he managed to shower. He looked…let's just say, like he'd run a marathon." She was grinning. "You know what, I'm going to sign off for now and let him sleep. I'll think about Caspian. I don't want to just boot him and tip our hand, but hell if I know what we *should* do."

"Likewise," Jay said glumly. "All right, I'll think it over as well and text you if I come up with anything. And Gracie?"

"Yeah?"

"Hang in there."

Gracie smiled. "I will. I'm glad you're here."

"Always," Jay said. He logged off and smiled at the screen, but his expression faded after a moment.

Someday, he thought, he was going to have to work up the courage to tell her that life was just better when she was around. Hell, sometimes he could barely sleep because he wanted to text that to her, or Skype her, or just log in to hear her voice.

But the thought of telling her that made him want to throw up.

He went off to the kitchen to get a glass of water and

stared at the wall as he drank it. "Don't be a fucking coward, Jay," he said when he was finished.

If only it were that easy. The phone was in his pocket, but if something that simple worked, he'd have sent the damned text already. He gave a little laugh and shook his head. He'd thought when he grew up, he'd have everything figured out. Turned out that was a crock of shit.

CHAPTER TWENTY

W hen Dragon Soul Productions had put in a gym, Dan reflected, they had thought it would help them attract and retain employees. Good work-life balance, holistic life goals, all that crap. Now he was using it for the exactly opposite purpose: he was showering there instead of going home and sleeping on the floor of his study.

It was the sort of thing you did when you found yourself in an unexpected cat-and-mouse game with a former colleague.

When he arrived back at his office, Dhruv was there, staring out the window. A few containers on the desk held homemade Indian food and one clean plate. A dirty one showed that Dhruv had already eaten. The smell of fresh chapatis made Dan's mouth water.

Dhruv looked around and nodded to the food. "Hope you don't mind that I dug in." With a rare flash of humor, he added, "Don't tell my mother. She'd hit me with a spoon if she knew I didn't give the guest the first serving."

Dan smiled. After a shower, and with the delicious food in front of him, he could try to forget everything that was going on. Homemade food from Dhruv's mother had been one of the highlights of office life since he'd finally convinced his parents to move to the US from Goa six months ago.

He loaded his plate with rice, prawn curry, *bhaji*, chapatis, and *tondak*, and dug in.

Dhruv stared out the window while Dan ate, only once looking over to snort and shake his head at Dan's makeshift taco: curry and rice wrapped in a chapati and topped with chutney. Dhruv, like most Indians Dan had met, was baffled by this American way of eating curry. After Dan finished his food, the two men exchanged looks.

"All right," Dhruv said, taking the guest chair across from Dan. "So, Harry's in the game."

Dan sighed. He was glad Dhruv had said it. *Not* saying it, *waiting* for someone to have the courage to say it—and thus make it real—had been a constant weight on his mind for the past two days. Despite the gut punch of the knowledge, it felt better to have it out in the open.

"He's in the game," Dan agreed.

They had both seen the fight. Whatever wizardry Harry had done meant that they couldn't hear the conversation between him and Callista, but it was clear that the two were no longer allies.

There was a long pause while the two men considered.

"I think he used the NPC GM port," Dhruv said finally. He was referring to the plug-in GMs could use to take control of one of the game's NPCs, which they had built to observe player interactions. "I don't think that boss was meant to be *him*, I think he just used it that way once he knew she was there."

Dan's mind skipped through the logic of what Dhruv was saying. "So you think he doesn't want her doing this quest," he said slowly.

"Yes. And I think if she fails any one fight, that's it. Otherwise, why bother fighting her? Why risk going into the game where we could see him?"

Dan sat back in his chair. After days of snacks from the break room, he'd been overly glad of a home-cooked meal, and he'd eaten far too much prawn curry. He was now absurdly full, and more than a little bit sleepy.

He rubbed his face. "Is this the sleep deprivation talking, or should we let them duke it out?"

Dhruv laughed. "Maybe I should have just ordered a pot of coffee instead of bringing food."

"We're past coffee now," Dan said philosophically. "Red Bull IV drip or nothing." He leaned on the desk. "But that's it, isn't it? We tweak the game slightly, nothing he'd notice, to make him a bit stronger and her a bit weaker. Then the next time they meet…"

"But we don't know where that will be," Dhruv pointed out.

Dan groaned.

To his surprise, Dhruv didn't look displeased. Instead, the other man was smiling slightly. "He's losing it," Dhruv said. "He knew we were keeping an eye on her, and he still risked letting us know he was in there." His tone turned gloating. "He never could control his temper. I don't know why we were worried."

"We were worried because he's a vengeful asshole and

the odds are pretty high of him burning the whole thing down if this doesn't go his way," Dan shot back.

Dhruv's careless smile evaporated, and he sighed. He nodded. "Right."

"We need to pick a side," Dan stated.

Dhruv gave him a heavy-lidded smile. "I'm guessing you have opinions."

"Yes. Unfortunately, they conflict." Dan stood up and stretched before starting to pace. If he kept sitting, he was going to fall asleep. "She's demonstrably less dangerous than he is. She doesn't know the architecture of the game, she can't access the databases, and just from a statistical likelihood standpoint, she's not as much of a fucking psychopath as Harry is."

Dhruv started laughing. "It would be a really big coincidence if she was," he agreed. He took a squeeze toy from Dan's desk and started throwing it up in the air and catching it. "But?"

"But we can't figure out how to get rid of her powers, and if her losing a fight to Harry could accomplish that, we'd have a shot of getting rid of two problems at once." Dan looked over his shoulder as he paced.

"You really like risky plans, don't you?" Dhruv rolled his eyes.

"No, I by far prefer situations where there don't need to be risky plans." Dan sat down. "But here we find ourselves." He heaved a sigh and tracked the squeeze toy as Dhruv kept throwing it.

"I have a question," Dhruv said. He caught the squeeze toy and didn't throw it again, his eyes locking on Dan's. "Why did you stick around? Here, I mean. When everything started to go to hell, why not just bail? Harry wasn't *your* roommate. You didn't really care about the game."

Dan felt his pride prickle. Dhruv was needling him, but there was no way to know if he was going for that or just being blunt.

And Dan didn't particularly like his answer to this.

"Fine. No, I didn't care," he said, "in terms of what it was. You two were the ones who cared about it that way. But I put a lot of work in. I deserved more than to be shoved out just because he felt like his *idea* should trump me making it real. I didn't want him to win."

Dhruv laughed. "I wondered," he admitted. "You don't advertise it, but you have a temper. You're more than happy to stand aside and let someone else win—unless they screw you over. Then you dig in your heels, and there is *no* moving you."

"Yeah, well." Dan forced a smile. "If we could *not* do a deep-dive into my psyche, that would be great. It's not like you're especially rational when it comes to these things."

"I am." Dhruv's smile disappeared. He leaned forward, intent now. "I am very, very rational. *Metamorphosis* is important."

Dan frowned. "I'm not saying it's not important—"

"No, I mean, to the world."

Dan paused. Dhruv wasn't much for hyperbole, so all Dan could think was that this was a deadpan joke of some kind. After all, it had all the hallmarks of a really bad one—or maybe a B movie script.

C movie, really.

But Dhruv didn't crack a smile. "You don't get it," he said seriously. "And that's fine. You've always just wanted to make the game good and keep it running, and you've been a good partner for that. But the game is important for what it *is*."

"And what is that, exactly?" He was still pretty sure this was a joke. Dan settled back in his chair and frowned.

Dhruv sighed. "A moral testing ground," he said finally.

"*Que?*"

"Don't make jokes. I'm serious. Do you know why people read books? Why they play games, watch movies? Why humans like stories?"

"Let's say no." Dan had never really thought about that.

"Because they teach us how to survive," Dhruv said. "It's how we pass down knowledge to one another. How you are going to make it through a battle or a storm, or whatever. You learn from stories. But now that we have video games, people can do something new: they can test things. They can see *why* we don't do certain things. They can start a war and see how much devastation it causes. They can stab someone in the back and feel the guilt."

Dan's frown deepened. He had never thought about this.

"Have you ever wanted something?" Dhruv asked him, "*Really* wanted it, but it was something you shouldn't have? A crush on your brother's girlfriend? Hell, craving some food you were allergic to?"

Dan shrugged. "Yeah."

"And maybe you didn't do anything because you thought through the implications and realized it was a bad idea?"

"Yeah, but that didn't always work."

"*Exactly.*" Dhruv stabbed his finger at the desk. "And

that's why this is important. We set up a world that we weren't messing with. They could do what they wanted. They could make alliances. They could break them. They could start wars. And Harry wants to mess with that. He wants to control it, because he can't accept that people fantasize about doing things they'd never do in real life. Things they *shouldn't* do in real life, and would be less likely to do if they could watch them play out."

Dan considered this, and he nodded. "So you two weren't just fighting about a game," he said finally.

"No," Dhruv said. "We were never just fighting about a game. He wanted to try to control people, and I wanted to let them learn that they didn't actually want to do terrible things."

Dan didn't say anything.

"So?" Dhruv asked.

"I'm thinking." Dan looked out the window. He was very tired now. He just wanted this to be over. But that was the way someone thought just before they lost, and he was *not* going to lose to Harry. "Can you remember which areas Harry worked on?" he asked Dhruv. "Before we decide what to do, we should get as much information as we can. We have to know where Harry and Callista might fight next, and go from there."

As for the rest, he'd be turning it over in his head. But he knew one thing for sure: if someone were to try to control the world and control people's choices, he damned sure wouldn't want it to be Harry.

He swiveled over to his laptop and typed up a quick message, and instead of the evasive response he expected, there was a knock on his office door a few moments later.

"Come in." Dan tilted his head to the side as Sam slipped into the room.

He knew Sam didn't approve of what the two of them were doing. It wasn't difficult to tell, although Dan had tolerated it. Sam rarely slid into outright rebellion, and he was a popular manager. Firing Jay had been difficult enough. Fire Sam and they might lose half their GMs.

"Yes?" Dan asked.

"You said you wanted to know all of the areas Harry worked on?" Sam asked.

"Yes." Dan tilted his head to the side as Sam hesitated.

"I wasn't here when Harry was here," Sam said finally. "I would normally just ask someone on the team for help, but they're a bit nervous with everything that's been going on."

"Ah." Dan looked at Dhruv. Neither of them had worked in ways that intersected Harry's work very much, even at the end. Now they were both regretting it. "I'll handle finding the information, then," he told Sam.

Sam hesitated again. "If I might make a suggestion," he began quietly. He seemed to be steeling himself for a fight.

"Yes?" Dan didn't bother to make his voice welcoming. He wasn't in the mood for an argument right now.

"She might be willing to help you," Sam said finally. He twisted his hands together and then blew out a long breath to steady himself. He looked at Dan, resigned. "She submitted a ticket when this all started. She thought it was a glitch. We're assuming she's out to screw us when the ones demanding special treatment are actually Demon Syndicate—"

"Enough." Dan's voice rose. He hated that, but he

wanted this to end. He forced a smile. "Thank you for your input, but this decision is made."

Sam left silently.

"Was he right?" Dan asked.

"No." Dhruv shrugged. "It's not like we're *doing* anything to her, and we make money how we make money. If he doesn't like it, he can leave."

"That's what I'm worried about," Dan muttered. He went back to searching the database, throwing one last raised eyebrow in Dhruv's direction. "So, are you going to help me find Harry's code or are you just going to sit there and talk about morals?"

"There's the Dan I know," Dhruv said with a grin. He stood up with a sigh. "I'll go start looking."

CHAPTER TWENTY-ONE

Gracie looked at the expanse of paper on the kitchen table and frowned. She'd been meticulous about planning her run of Yesuan's Haunt, but she knew that it was useless. Anxiety was a constant throb in the background of her mind.

Had she not planned well enough? It was possible. She paced around the outside edge of the table, looking down at the hand-drawn map. She'd recreated it from the information available online, and had come up with the best ways to defeat every known mob, patrol, and boss in the place.

None of them were particularly tricky, but there was one dilemma she couldn't resolve: Caspian. Dathok's trial run as an assassin had shown that DPS was where his talents truly lay. He had a real talent for knowing when and how to strike, and he had a natural affinity for creating combos.

With Caspian on board to back up Alan, the team was

much more solid. Now that they knew Caspian was from Demon Syndicate, that was hardly a surprise, though.

Bringing Dathok back in as their secondary healer would make them weaker, and likelier to wipe and lose the quest for good, but using Caspian was like waiting for someone to stab her in the back. She still hadn't said anything to him, not wanting Demon Syndicate or Dragon Soul to know she was onto them.

Or that was what she told herself. In reality, she hadn't spoken to Caspian because she was hurt. They'd helped him, run dungeons with him, gathered crafting materials, and talked about game philosophy.

No wonder he'd seemed to fit in so well. It hadn't been because he was a good fit. It was because he was doing anything he could to earn their trust.

She rubbed her head and tried to clear her mind by going through the raid again step by step. Yesuan had been banished to spend eternity alone, but he had managed to draw creatures of darkness to him over the eons: imps, spectres, and even the fallen angels who had made the Aosi and were determined to see them prevail.

The first part of the run was designed to test reflexes, pitting the team against the booby traps Yesuan had surrounded himself with. Some were mechanized defenders, hurling insults in automated voices, and some were effects that dealt damage to those standing in certain areas, or wounds that the healers must scramble to deal with before the next trap. Even when you knew the patterns, they could be difficult to execute.

After that, the team would find themselves dealing with Oryxa, a succubus who had joined his cause for reasons unknown. Gracie, who tried to learn the lore behind a dungeon without hearing any particular spoilers or seeing the boss's cinematics, was particularly interested in Oryxa. She knew why Yesuan had fallen to darkness, but why were the creatures of darkness helping him?

She'd know soon, she supposed. She just wished she could spend her time looking forward to this, knowing that if the team wiped, it would be no big deal rather than knowing that if they wiped, she might lose something that had transformed her life.

The founders of Dragon Soul had tried to screw her again and again. If she lost the protection Harry had unintentionally given her, she might be banned from the game.

She couldn't let that happen.

She hunched her shoulders as she stared at the rest of the papers. She knew them by heart. A trail of imps and minor demons would lead to Yesuan, and he was flanked by two fallen angels. It was impossible to destroy Yesuan without killing both of the angels first, but Yesuan would continue to attack the group while they burned the angels down, meaning that it was imperative both to finish that stage of the fight quickly and to interrupt his attacks.

Caspian had an ability that could interrupt another healer's spell-casting.

Gracie shook her head, then looked at the door with a sigh. If Alex were here, they could bat ideas back and forth over a pizza or some Thai food, and he could give her his opinion on whether or not to trust Caspian.

But Alex, of course, wasn't here. He was off, moving on with his life and being a successful adult while Gracie sat alone in the dark and stressed about playing video games.

She rubbed her forehead and sighed. Every day she got a little closer to packing all of her stuff up, hiring a moving truck, and going…

She didn't know where she would go.

But at times like these, it didn't seem like a terrible idea.

"Bingo," Dhruv said three hours later.

He had tracked down every email he could find that mentioned Harry's work. Some were complaints from associates, mentioning that Harry was a pain to work with and wouldn't take their suggestions. Some were from Harry, annoyed about the "incompetence" of those same employees. One or two were the rare written acknowledgment between Dan and Dhruv, still carefully coded, that they were giving Harry fake projects to keep him out of their hair.

Or, at least, that was what they had *thought* they were doing. In reality, they had wound up giving him free rein to put this quest line in the game.

The emails that made him stop for a moment were the oldest ones, the ones that had been full of excitement and ideas. Back at the start, it had been all late nights in the dorm room, sandwiches smuggled out of the dining hall and sodas from the vending machine, and then a barely-furnished apartment with whole cases of ramen in the corner of the main room and mattresses on the floor with clothes piled beside them, staying up until all hours to sketch out their ideas for zones and bosses.

In those days, the difference in their two world views

hadn't seemed insurmountable. They'd even thought it was *good*, in a way—that no matter what people came to the game to find, they'd find it. Although they tended to yell when they debated, it had all been in good fun.

Dhruv sat back in his chair, his brow furrowed. If he were honest with himself, he'd have to say that he genuinely missed Harry. The man could be an asshole, but *damn* if he didn't make every project more fun.

And they wouldn't be here if Harry hadn't dreamed up *Metamorphosis Online*.

Dhruv shook his head. Harry had given them something useful, yes, but the friendship was gone. Harry had decided it was his way or the highway. He hadn't left Dan and Dhruv any other choice than to do things this way.

Now Dhruv's only real option was to use Harry's words against him.

So he'd spent his time combing back through the things Harry had spoken about—the ideas about whether superior beings could ever be an effective tool for gods to use? Leadership should be a figurehead or something to unite the people *against*.

It was that last one that provided the necessary clue. Only one zone explored the idea that the best leader might be one who was universally hated, and that zone was Yesuan's Haunt. And there, lurking in the battle scripts, Dhruv found it: the piece that would allow Harry to get in and control the quest.

And what they could use to cut him off once he'd served his purpose.

Dhruv smiled sadly as he typed out a message to Dan. He'd almost enjoyed this cat-and-mouse game they were playing, although he would never tell Dan that, and now it was drawing to a close.

All things must end, however.

Jamie wrapped a towel around his waist and dried his hair, running his fingers through it afterward to smooth it back out. He hadn't been keeping up with his usual routine in the past few weeks, and his hair was longer than it had been in years. He'd shaved today for the first time in a while, and although his face now felt more familiar, the bare skin was oddly itchy.

He headed back to his room, jumping when he opened the door to find Thad slouched in the desk chair.

Thad gave him a nod and stood. "I'll go so you can get dressed, but I just wanted you to know to be quick. Dragon Soul has something they want you to do."

Jamie groaned but nodded. "I'll be glad when this is over," he said in response to Thad's questioning look. "I'm really over it."

"Yeah," Thad agreed. "I get that. Seems like we're getting there, though. Anyway, I'll see you in the conference room."

He left, whistling, and Jamie changed as quickly as he could without thinking about anything at all. He didn't want to guess what they were going to have him do. Get Callista on tape saying she was breaking the rules, maybe?

He shook his head. Even though he clung to the belief that she *must* be lying, he didn't like deceiving her and her team. He just wanted this to be done.

When he arrived at the conference room with a granola bar and a mug of lukewarm coffee, two of the BrightStar team were there with Thad. Evan gave Jamie a nod, and Evan's boss, Frank, also nodded brusquely, although he barely looked up from his paperwork. Frank had made no secret of the fact that he didn't like sponsoring a competitive gaming team, and he was always doing other business during these meetings.

On the screen were two of the three Dragon Soul founders, who Jamie had never seen in the flesh before. They had done calls, but never a video chat. He was surprised to see how young the two men looked. They must be worth millions of dollars apiece at this point and had to be pushing forty, but they had a youthful look to them.

"You're Jamie?" Dhruv asked. "Thank you for your help so far."

Jamie nodded. "It was in everyone's interest," he said. It was the sort of thing you were supposed to say, right? But no one seemed to think very well of it. Frank grimaced—although he could be grimacing at anything, Jamie supposed—and the two Dragon Soul founders did little more than nod.

"After this is over, I'd be interested in your take on the different guild structures," Dan said. "But that's not important right now. What *is* important is that we need Callista to run Yesuan's Haunt, and you need to go along. She *has* to wipe on that run. Just once; that's all we need."

Jamie frowned. "What?" This didn't seem like much to ask, in his opinion. How often did guilds wipe on dungeon runs, after all? It was obscenely common when learning new content.

"We have reason to believe—" Dhruv began, but Dan cut in.

"That's all," he said simply. Of the two, he was clearly the business partner. "As you're thinking, this isn't an unusual thing to have happen. We simply need to make *sure* that it will. We need you on the run, and we need you to see if you can finagle them into taking an unusual setup."

Jamie frowned.

"As you've heard and seen," Dan said patiently, "sometimes Callista's team encounters unusual bosses. It would make sense to believe that the same would happen this time, so it shouldn't be difficult to have her stack the team differently."

"What if I stack it the wrong way?" Jamie said impatiently.

"You won't. As far as we can tell, all she'll encounter this time is the normal set of bosses." Dan smiled tightly.

Jamie considered this for a long moment. "She's won in situations you thought she'd wipe in before," he pointed out. "How can you be *sure?*"

"We can't be. That's why we need you to go." Dan's voice sounded a little strained now. "We're forcing through a patch later in the day that will make the fights more difficult. Just try to keep people alive until you get to the final boss, and then let them wipe."

Jamie nodded silently.

"Do you have concerns?" It was Dhruv who spoke this time. He was looking intently at Jamie.

"Not specifically," Jamie said. He forced a smile. "We're close to figuring this out, right? Then it will be over?"

"Yes," Dan confirmed. "You can go back to your team. We have no specific quarrel with any member of her team, so if there are people you've enjoyed playing with, I'm sure they could apply to be part of Demon Syndicate."

Thad's face got almost purple at the thought. Jamie looked away hastily and nodded.

"I'll get that going," he said. "You'll want a heads-up when we go in, right?"

"Sure," Dan said. "As always, Jamie, thank you for your help." His voice was dry. "We couldn't have done this without all of you."

He ended the call, and Jamie looked at Thad.

"It's accepted to send moles into rival guilds, isn't it?" Evan asked worriedly. Beside him, Frank didn't seem to have noticed that the call had ended.

"Yes," Thad said impatiently. "They're just giving us shit because we went over their heads to do it. They screwed us over, though, so they owe us. They can't throw too big a tantrum." He stood and nodded to Jamie. "The sooner you do this, the sooner it's all over."

"Yeah," Jamie said, standing up as well. "Could be back to normal life by tomorrow. I like that idea." He headed off with a two-finger salute to Thad and a nod to Evan.

CHAPTER TWENTY-TWO

It wasn't just Alex who wasn't home or online. *Everyone*, from Alan to Dathok, seemed to have something or other going on today. Even Jay was offline, exhausted from another late night of scouting at Night's Edge. What secrets still remained in that zone, Gracie wasn't sure, but she was now *dreaming* of the alleys and buildings, seeing their imprints behind her eyes.

She'd planned the Yesuan's Haunt run alone, and now, with no one around to talk to, she was making her way through a particularly gnarly section of the Ocru homeland. The Ocru and the Piskies, it turned out, had managed to stay intertwined within one another's lore even after the races were scattered. The Piskies had a bunch of statues to the Ocru, whom they had believed were gods, and the Ocru seemed to think the Piskies were some sort of cross between a house spirit and the protective aegis of their ancestors.

As a result, this zone was dotted with knee-high statues

and absurdly tiny "houses" that had been constructed for the "spirits."

She really, really wanted Kevin to come out here so she could take screenshots of his character in the tiny houses. So far, he was claiming that it would be too big an assault on his dignity, an assertion Gracie did not believe in the slightest.

Anyone that concerned about their dignity was *not* going to be playing a two-foot-tall character, almost half the height of which was a bright pink hairdo.

She'd get him out here one of these days.

In the meantime, she was going to kill some lizard people. They'd taken over these ruins since the Ocru began returning to Kithara, and the Ocru had asked passing adventurers for help.

Gracie was only too happy to oblige.

A hiss and a rattle let her know that one of the lizard people was nearby, and she spun and ducked in one fluid motion, barely avoiding a spear that went over her head. There was a stab of adrenaline in her stomach, the instinctive reaction that told her that someone was *trying to stab her with a goddamned spear* and she needed to get the hell out of the way.

The lizard person hissed at her again, and Gracie launched out of her crouch without a pause. She smiled as she felt the power in her legs now. When she was in high school, everything had been focused on how thin she was or whether she was showing too much skin, or too little.

Never in her life had she focused on how *strong* she was, and it felt amazing. She'd been playing around with the idea of trying to figure out how to lift weights so she could have strong arms to match her newly-strong legs, but she couldn't imagine admitting to a personal trainer that her leg strength was from playing video games.

She felt her phone buzz as she leveled a flurry of punches at the lizard's midsection, and then followed them up with some knee strikes and kicks. By the end of the fight, she was panting, and she'd forgotten about the phone —until it buzzed again. Gracie hurriedly checked the number on the screen, frowning when she saw Kevin's info.

She seriously considered not answering it. He was probably just checking in on her after her call the other day, and she wasn't in a much better place right now. Part of her was embarrassed about leaning on anyone, ever, and she felt guilty for calling Kevin that day, even though she knew he hadn't minded.

Still…

She sighed, logged out hurriedly, and called him back.

"Hey, what's up?" She tried to keep her voice light.

"Did you listen to my message?"

"No, I was in the game."

"Ah." Kevin sounded like he was frowning. "Um, I was supposed to pass a phone number on to you. Someone contacted Alan and told him to pass the number to me to pass to you. I just… I don't know who it is, and neither does he."

Gracie dropped her helmet, resisting the urge to kick it across the room. The lizard people should be glad she wasn't logged in anymore because she'd be tearing them a new one if she was. "Son of—that horse-buggered, spineless, petty-as-fuck, *dickless*—"

"Uh…do you mind telling me who you're talking about?" Kevin was laughing now. "I know I shouldn't laugh. I do. You're clearly angry, but I *have* to know who's got you this upset."

"Harry," Gracie said through gritted teeth. "The guy who came up with the idea for *Metamorphosis Online*. He was supposed to be the one with the shiny gold armor and the ranking, and now he's trying to intimidate me into giving it all up so he can run the game as some sort of god-emperor."

"Oh, fuck that," Kevin said promptly. "Gracie for god-empress or no dice. Let me know how many votes you need."

That, at least, made her laugh. She headed over to the couch, still panting, and flopped down.

"But I don't know why it would be him," Kevin said after a moment.

Gracie frowned up at the ceiling. "Actually, that's a good point. Why *would* he go through all that trouble? He knows where I live, so I'm sure he could get my number. Why…" She sighed. "Did you or Alan try calling it?"

"Yes, but whoever it was, they didn't pick up." He was regretful. "I seriously thought about not telling you, but I thought you'd want to know."

Gracie nodded thoughtfully, then realized he couldn't see that. "No, that was a good call, don't worry. Okay. I'll call and…see what happens, I guess. You'll text it to me?"

"I suppose." Kevin sounded unsure now. "Gracie, are you sure this is safe? Is anyone home with you?"

Gracie started laughing. "What, do you think it's something like *The Ring,* and a demon is going to climb out of my phone?"

"No. I'm not crazy, but if people are showing up at your house…"

"I'll call you once I know who it is," Gracie promised. "Look, I'll text first, okay? Then I can keep you updated at the same time."

"Thanks. Be safe." He ended the call.

Gracie sighed as she waited for his text to come in, then sent a brief text to the new number, frowning.

Who is this?

The answer came back almost at once. **Is this Callista?**

Yes. She was too angry to lie. **Who the hell is this?**

It's Caspian. There was a pause while the person texted, deleted what they were typing, then repeated the whole exercise. Finally, a brief message appeared.

We need to talk.

Gracie stared at the far wall, her heart pounding. She didn't doubt that this was Caspian, but she hadn't wanted this confrontation today. She hadn't wanted to have this out.

I'm not sure what we have to talk about, she texted back finally.

Can I Skype you? Caspian asked. **Face to face so you can see I'm being honest. I have to tell you something**. There was a pause, and then he added, as if worried she wouldn't agree, **It's about your quest. Dragon Soul wants you to fail it**.

Gracie frowned down at the screen. She dashed off a quick message to Kevin as she thought, and then she said, **Fine. I'll send you my screen name.**

A few minutes later, she was sitting cross-legged on the couch, scowling as Caspian started the call.

To her surprise, when he answered, he was in his mid-twenties, and well put-together. He saw her skepticism.

"All the competitive gaming teams have to work out like crazy," he said. "We have *very* strict rules—curfews, almost no alcohol, and stuff like that. They tried cutting out caffeine once, but there was nearly a riot. Some of the guys are *unbearable* without it."

Gracie laughed despite herself. That was the thing about Caspian—even in the game, you *wanted* to like him. She wiped the smile off her face and stared him down. "You're from Demon Syndicate."

Well, the cat was out of the bag now. She'd never been very good at lying and playing games within games.

His eyebrows shot up. "You *knew*? Wait, how did you know? How long have you known?"

At least he didn't deny it.

"For a bit," Gracie said tightly. She tried to bite back the words, but they came out anyway. "You know what, man? Fuck you for doing that. Alan spent a whole bunch of time teaching you. We all tried to help you. And all we were doing was minding our own business. We didn't need that shit."

Caspian was quiet. He had looked around furtively as her voice rose, but now he shook his head.

"You weren't just minding your own business, though. You were going for the month-first. I'm not saying you shouldn't have, but you knew other people wanted it. You knew you were competing. This is what happens."

"Nice way to absolve yourself," Gracie spat back. "Someone was going to do it, so it might as well be you?"

"No!" he exploded finally. "I didn't want to! I wanted someone else to handle it. I just wanted you to leave my team the hell alone so things could go back to normal. I thought I was going to find out you had some crazy trick we could copy, and we'd steal it and be back on top. That was all! That was why I was there."

Gracie sat back, frowning.

"And then…" Caspian sighed. "Look, I didn't *want* to like you guys. You're casuals, and you just waltzed in and took something we worked *really* hard for."

Now Gracie could see where he was going. She gave a small smile, though it was bitter. "So you didn't *want* to sell us out," she said, "and you want my forgiveness. Well, shove it up your ass."

"*No.*" Caspian shook his head. "For fuck's sake, I'm trying to *help* you. They want you to fail this quest. They're tweaking the game tonight so Yesuan's Haunt will be a harder run. They think you'll see only the normal bosses, and they want me to talk you into taking some weird group configuration with you. They literally said, 'any weird configuration.'"

Gracie frowned at him. "You're not messing with me? You mean it?"

"I mean it." He shook his head. "I thought I was going to go along with it. I told myself that was why I was there. But…" He cleared his throat awkwardly. "I've had more fun playing the game with you guys than I ever did before. Honestly. It's just *fun* with you. And Alan *did* try to help me. You know how rare that is? Everyone was so nice. It…well, it was different."

Gracie considered this, then she let out a breath she hadn't realized she was holding. "Send me what you can," she said. "Over text, however you can. Tell me their plans."

"And…" Caspian looked uncertain.

"And I'll think hard about whether I want to trust you," Gracie said bluntly, reaching out to finish the call.

Her phone buzzed again and she glanced at it, doing a double take.

That quest was never meant to be yours, and you will not win. I created this world. Do you truly think you can beat me?

Gracie blinked for a moment. The message wasn't signed, but it hardly needed a signature. There was only one person who would be arrogant enough to send it—not to mention so arrogant that he wouldn't realize he was giving Gracie the final push she needed to claim this place in the world of *Metamorphosis*.

CHAPTER TWENTY-THREE

When Alex arrived home, Gracie was standing on the balcony, contemplatively eating Oreos two at a time.

Three at a time had turned out to be too messy.

"Hey," Alex said from the doorway.

"Hey." Gracie looked over her shoulder with a smile. "Heading out to dinner with Sydney?" She might feel lonely now that Alex was out and about so much, but when she saw how happy he was, she couldn't help but be glad. She'd seen the hint of sadness and loneliness in him—it was part of why she'd given Sydney his number—but she hadn't realized just *how* happy Alex was now that he had a crush.

It was good to see.

To her surprise, though, he grinned and held up a bag of takeout from her favorite Vietnamese restaurant. "Nope. We've spent most of the past week together, and we agreed it was time to remind our friends that we still love them."

"Awww." Gracie clasped her hands over her heart dramatically to cover the fact that she felt a bit misty-eyed at this revelation. "Well, aren't you guys sweet?"

"We thought so," Alex said smugly.

"Already using 'we,' are you? You're going to be a disgustingly cute couple, I can just tell." Gracie followed him into the kitchen, grinning.

Alex grabbed plates and silverware without saying anything, but there was a smile playing around his mouth, and when he put the plates on the table, he said quietly, "I hope so."

"Awwww!" Grace clutched at her heart again. "Look at that face! You're smitten! I am dying of cute. Holy crap, man."

"Yeah, yeah." Alex dumped some noodles onto his plate, trying unsuccessfully to glare at her. "Don't make a big deal of it."

"Oh, I am *totally* gonna make a big deal of it. You're so happy!" Gracie spooned some noodles onto her own plate. "For the first time in the history of ever for anyone, dipping their toe back into dating isn't a drama-filled clusterfuck. You won the jackpot, you know."

"I think so." Alex ate a bite of chicken. "Now I just have to get a job where I'm not beholden to self-important assholes."

"If you find out what kind of job that is, you tell me." Gracie stabbed her fork in his direction. "We could make good money selling that secret."

"Hmmm." Alex contemplated this. "All right, so how have *you* been?"

"What? I don't get to know all the lovey-dovey details?" Gracie got up and went to get them glasses of water.

"Not even a little bit," Alex called after her.

"Just my luck that you'd be all gentlemanly about this," she grumbled as she filled her glass. "I can't even disapprove without being a jerk. Bah. Well, fine." She came back and plunked the two glasses down. "I don't have any good news on my end, though. Shit hit the fan and it's a real bummer, so…"

Alex put his fork down. "Wait, what?"

"I, uh…" Gracie bit her lip. She was now very aware of just how much she hadn't told Alex. "Things went a little crazy."

She briefed Alex on the events of the past couple of weeks, watching as his eyes widened and his brows rose incredulously. By the time she was done, his jaw was hanging open, and he'd had a bite of chicken held up to it for the past two minutes. He dumped it off his fork and stared at her.

"So, uh…" He looked away for a moment, tapping the fork on his plate. "Uh…hmm. Holy shit."

"Yeah." Gracie started shoveling food into her mouth. She'd been talking for a while, and she had therefore been neglecting the amazing food Alex had brought home. It turned out that almost an entire package of Oreos was *not* a filling snack.

Her mother would be horrified to hear that, but then again…

"Oh, also, my mother is icing me out," Gracie said with a brittle smile. "She wants me to go play happy family at my sister's engagement party, and I don't want to. It's not like Katie wants me there, either. We've hardly seen eye to eye for a while, but my mom is *insisting...* Ugh, not important."

"Katie's the golden child," Alex pointed out. "So everyone has to *see* her win."

Gracie stared at him. "That's disgustingly true. I'd never thought about it that way. Seriously?"

"Gracie, you've got a life a ton of people would kill for," Alex told her. "Including *you*, a few months ago."

Gracie, who had been opening her mouth to retort, closed it again. "That's...also a good point. I've *missed* you, man. You give good advice."

"I know I do," Alex said serenely. "Look, you hated your job before—justifiably, I might add—and now you're making more than that from playing a video game with people you *like* hanging out with. I mean, aside from Caspian. I'm still not sure why you're not throwing him out on his ass."

"Me neither, honestly." Gracie finished her food and looked sadly at the empty plate.

"I think there's a black hole in your stomach," Alex informed her. "I'll have you know that when I ordered this much food, they asked if I was having a party. I didn't have the heart to tell them that my roommate was an open pit that food falls into and never escapes."

"You make me sound like a menace." Gracie licked her fork off and began cleaning up.

"Yeah. You've massacred *how* many packages of cookies this week alone?"

"I don't have to answer that," Gracie said with great dignity. She threw a smile over her shoulder. "Seriously, thank you for dinner. And for listening to me ramble."

"Yeah." Alex leaned back in his chair. "So, what are we going to do about Caspian, then?"

"*We?*" Gracie raised an eyebrow as she loaded the dishwasher.

"Hell, yeah. I'm playing with you all tonight, and maybe I'm gonna get Caspian alone in a dark alley and feed him to a giant spider." Alex gave an elaborate shrug. "It might happen. Totally by accident, I assure you."

Gracie snorted.

Alex got up and wandered over to the pile of papers in the corner. "Is this the research you did for the next dungeon run?"

"Yeah." Gracie chewed her lip. "And I honestly don't know whether we should run it. They're just waiting for us to do it—Harry is, *and* Dragon Soul. Maybe we just let them rot and go off and do other things."

Alex considered this silently as he scanned the documentation she'd put together.

"On the other hand," Gracie said, wandering around the living room with her hands in her pockets, "if Harry still wants the quest, he must think it's valuable. So, is it? Maybe it would protect me from Dragon Soul." She chewed her lip and admitted, "And part of me just wants to win because they so clearly don't want me to. *Real* mature."

Alex held up a finger. "But understandable."

"Ha. I'm glad you get me." Gracie flopped back onto the couch and curled up. "So, *if* Caspian can be trusted, we'll basically get the normal Yesuan's Haunt run. Which means, I guess, that Harry will be one of the normal end-bosses?"

"He's been able to take over bosses before, clearly." Alex brought the papers over. "What does Jay think?" He looked up in time to catch the evasive flicker in Gracie's eyes. "What? What happened? Did you two have a falling out?"

"No! No." Gracie shook her head. "I just…uh."

"Gracie. Wait, what's your middle name so I can middle-name you? Hell, what's your *full* name? Grace? Gracetopher?"

Gracie snorted water up her nose and mock-glared at him as she grabbed a paper towel. "Yes, my full name is Gracetopher. Nice that you remembered."

"I pay attention to things." He settled down in a chair. "So what happened with Jay?"

"I've just been a mess," Gracie burst out. "You're moving on and getting a girlfriend, and I'm happy for you. I *am*. It just makes me realize how much of a mess my own life is. I don't really have a career, my job is playing a video game that the creators are actively trying to throw me out of, and I have this crush…" She shook her head, her cheeks going pink. "You didn't hear that."

"Awww." Alex gave her a look.

"No." Gracie hid her face in her hands. "Stop. Stop looking at me like that."

"Gracie, you have a *crush*. So you've… Oh, I get it—you decided not ever to talk to him anymore so that you could… Uh, no, never mind. That makes *no sense at all*." He glared at her. "*None*."

"I know!" Gracie flailed her arms. "But I called Kevin to sob at him about being a total failure, and the last thing I want is for Jay to see me like that. I'm supposed to be running this guild. I'm supposed to be strong and have my shit together. People depend on me."

"Gracie." Alex sounded stricken. All of the humor dropped away and he reached out to take her hand, totally serious now. "We started playing this game for fun, and we liked playing with you because you made us laugh. We ran through dungeons and never expected to make it. We did a crazy shot-in-the-dark insane thing to make that month-first dungeon run. It wasn't like we really thought we'd become the top-rated guild or anything. When we made you guild leader, it wasn't supposed to make you crazy." He squeezed her hand.

Gracie squeezed back and managed a small smile.

"Seriously," Alex said. "If this is too much pressure on you…"

"It just fucking sucks!" The words came out of her sounding all strange, her voice blaring oddly. "I showed up in the game, and all of a sudden, people hated me. Like, *hated* me, Alex. I have some douche showing up at *my fucking house.* I have the people who run the game trying to ban my account. It's a mindfuck. I didn't ask for any of it. It just came out of fucking nowhere."

"I get that." Alex squeezed her hand again. "I'm going to murder Caspian. The last thing you needed was someone fucking with you even more."

"Ughhhh." Gracie tipped her head back. "That's the thing. Do I trust him? At all?"

Alex thought about this for a while. He settled back in his chair, spinning the bottle of beer in his hands and staring into space.

"I'd almost say yes," he said finally. "Actually."

Gracie frowned at him.

"It would have been easier not to tell you anything," Alex said. "You said he really didn't seem to know that you had found out who he was. *That* means that if he wanted to keep lying, he'd have just said nothing, right?"

Gracie nodded. She got up and began to stretch, reaching for her toes. She'd found out the hard way that if she didn't stretch at the end of the day now, her tired muscles would get very tight while she slept and she'd spend the next day hobbling around like a caricature of an old person.

She stretched out her arms to place her hands flat on the floor and slowly lengthened her back, feeling the backs of her legs gradually loosen.

"I thought he liked hanging out with us," she said finally. "We ran that one dungeon against Harry and everything went to shit, and Jay said that Caspian was just loving the hell out of it, throwing heals around and cheering people on. He seemed like our kind of people."

"Maybe he *is*," Alex said. "Just for a second, take his story at face value. Does it hang together? Does it fit with what you know of him that he would infiltrate the group and then realized he actually enjoyed being there?"

Gracie thought about this as she rotated her shoulders, stretching one side and then the other. "Yeah," she said finally. Blood was building up in her head and she stood up, wincing through the rush. "Yeah, honestly, it does."

"So it could be true," Alex said quietly. "It makes a lot of sense, and telling you would be much riskier than just letting you go in on your own. Hell, he could even have sat this one out to put you at ease, but no, he *told* you what was going on. Gracie, I think he's for real."

Gracie sighed. "So…"

"So you figure out what *you* want," Alex said. "Not what you think *we* want. What *you* want. Do you want to run this guild? Do you want to beat Harry?"

A sense of purpose pulsed through her. Gracie picked up her head to stare at him. "Yes," she said fiercely. "Yes, I do. I don't know whether I want to be some crazy empress or whatever, but I know I want to protect the game from those jackasses because they'll rip it apart if they get the chance."

"Good," Alex said decisively.

"So I'll tell people that," Gracie said. "I'll tell, uh…Jay." She felt her cheeks get hot. "But should I tell him the rest?"

"Maybe take this thing one battle at a time," Alex said, reaching out to pat her hand. "Once we've done this dungeon run, you can tackle the next problem, okay?"

"Good call." Gracie felt a rush of relief. "I'm not nearly brave enough to tell him, so that was the right answer."

"Given what I've seen of you two together…" Alex began.

"What?" Gracie looked at him.

"Nothing. Let's focus on one thing at a time." He nodded at the VR headsets. "I'll start texting people. Once we log in, I think we can assume we'll be on the clock, so as much as we can do outside their systems, we should do."

"Oh. Right." Gracie wiped her palms on her jeans. "Now. We're doing it right now. I, uh…"

"Don't give yourself time to overthink it," Alex advised.

"You've done your research, now trust your instincts and *go* for it."

Gracie gave a determined nod. "Right. Let's see when we can get people online, brief them, and then go."

"With Caspian?" Alex asked curiously. His tone made it clear that this was her choice. He simply wanted to see what she would pick.

Gracie hesitated. "Yeah," she said finally. "With Caspian. I'll text him last."

CHAPTER TWENTY-FOUR

Jay wasn't sure how many times he'd opened his messages to send Gracie a text and then closed the app without doing so.

Hey, are you all right?

Haven't heard from you in a while. Everything okay?

Harry hasn't been back, has he?

Please tell me you're all right.

He hadn't sent her any messages, though. He knew what was going on, after all. She was occupied with more important things. She was hanging out with her family, or she'd gotten a new job, or—

Or she had a boyfriend now. Jay always felt a sick drop of dread in his stomach when he thought of that. It wasn't exactly unlikely, was it? Gracie was drop-dead gorgeous. All she'd have to do was go to the grocery store, and she could have five new boyfriends by the time she got home.

She'd probably stab him if she heard him say that, though. Even *thinking* it seemed risky. He looked over his shoulder to make sure she wasn't right there.

Then his phone buzzed and he saw her name on the notification, and his stomach flip-flopped and completely disappeared. He could hear a buzzing in his ears. She'd texted. About what, though?

Yesuan's Haunt. Get people together, send texts as much as possible, send me a message telling me who you get hold of. We'll load in together and start the run.

He sat bolt upright. One kind of nerves was replaced by another. Gracie was going to run the final dungeon in the quest—because Jay believed whole-heartedly that it *was* the final stage. When she finished this, she'd be untouchable.

She just had to get past Harry first.

And Dragon Soul.

He texted back, **Roger**. A moment later, he added, **Look, I don't want to be a downer, but what are the odds that they pull the servers down?**

There was a pause. She started typing, then stopped. Started again. Stopped. Finally:

Sam?

That was it—just one word. Jay pondered, pictured exactly what series of curses Sam was going to level at him when he asked for this, and then decided to go for it anyway. Sam could always say no, after all.

He just wasn't going to.

On it, he told Gracie.

Right. There was a pause while she typed, **I'm going to bring Caspian in with us. I'll explain after. I think he's on our side.**

Jay raised his eyebrows but decided not to second-guess her. They had enough stacked against them now; she wouldn't make this choice lightly. **Okay**, he typed.

He sent off a few messages to the team, asking Kevin to continue spreading the word, and then gave a sigh and called Sam.

Sam didn't pick up right away, so Jay waited. He paced back and forth and was just considering getting in his car and driving to the Dragon Soul offices when his phone rang. He smiled slightly and picked up.

"What's going on?" Sam began before Jay could even say hi.

"We need a distraction," Jay said at once. "We're doing a run, and need them not to notice. Can you hold a strategy meeting or something?" There was a very long pause, but Jay said nothing. He knew that trying to cajole Sam would backfire. Sam was weighing the options, and he would make what he thought was the right decision.

"I'll come up with something," he said finally. "Give me an hour."

"An hour?" Jay could only imagine them all waiting, twiddling their thumbs.

"An hour." Sam was adamant. "Take it or leave it."

"No, no, an hour's fine. Sorry. Thanks, Sam."

"Yeah, yeah. And instead of a nice bottle of Scotch for Christmas, maybe you could get me a new job?" Sam sounded wryly amused. "Since I'm pretty sure I'm going to need one." He sighed. "I'll send a text when I can."

Sam hung up and sighed again. There were a few ways of distracting people in offices, but he had learned the most effective one a while back. Nothing else even came close to this particular strategy. He sent two texts, made a call, and then went to do the other step he needed to do while he waited for his strategy to unfold.

Dan and Dhruv had alerts set up to tell them when Callista logged into the game. These alerts had occasionally not worked, and Sam briefly considered unhooking them, but then he thought of a better way to go about things.

The interoffice email system had been designed by a former employee who was very good at building databases and very bad at building email systems. It worked. Sometimes. When it felt like it. The rest of the time, the teams used various chat programs.

But it was this email system that sent the alerts to Dan and Dhruv, and Sam knew he could use that to his advantage.

First, he set up a cache to harness any alerts that *did* come in about Callista, then he set the system to cycle at unstable intervals. With the system going down a lot, he knew that Dan and Dhruv would be glued to their phones, waiting for alerts that weren't ever going to show up. And in the meantime…

"Sam?" One of his employees stuck his head into the room. "Pizza's here, and Ruchir says he's on his way back with the donuts and coffee. Also…" He gave a meaningful nod. Sam had told him to spread the word that no one was to mention if they saw Callista's team log in, and all of them were to set their screens to watch different guilds.

"Awesome." Sam stood up and strolled into the main room. "Hey, everyone, I know it's been a stressful few weeks. Make sure to get up, stretch a bit, and have some food. You know what? Paul, see if you can work out a schedule to get people home early in shifts for the next few days."

People clapped and swarmed over to the pizza.

"Oh, hey." Sam looked at one of the newer people. "You know, Dan and Dhruv have been working long hours too. Could you go let them know there's food?"

"Sure." The newbie looked wide-eyed, but he trotted off to get the two founders.

Sam took a slice of pizza and gave a grim smile. Between email troubles, blocked alerts, and pizza, he was as confident as he could be that Dan and Dhruv wouldn't know about the run until it was too late to stop it. He pulled out his phone and typed a quick text.

You're on. Go now.

Gracie had sent a cascade of texts explaining the Yesuan's Haunt run from start to finish. Caspian, having been a part of Demon Syndicate, already knew the details, and she wanted him to be as surprised as possible.

The less time he had to turn on them, the better.

Right now she was running through the fight with Yesuan.

Now, Yesuan can't be killed while Azrael and Lirael are still alive, she typed out. This message was being sent to Kevin and Alan, who were sending the messages on to others. **And he'll back them up. His main mechanic is interrupts**.

Is there any warning on them? Alan asked.

Yes, and it's doubly important, because on the third

interrupt, he'll follow up with an AoE stun and then follow THAT up with a strong AoE damage spell. People HAVE to scatter as soon as they see him gearing up for interrupt number 3. Drop whatever they're doing. The signal is he'll yell, "Your spells have no power here." We're going to put Alex on the count.

Got it, Kevin typed back.

Azrael is vulnerable to holy magic, so Caspian and Alan will need to both heal and do holy corrupts on him. We don't have any paladins, but I have some holy damage from my new shield, so I'll be on Azrael, and Lakhesis will tank Lirael. Lirael is vulnerable to fire, so brief Ushanas on that, and Alex will be doing fire enchants on his arrows.

Her phone buzzed with a message from Jay: **Sam says go NOW.**

Roger. To Alan and Kevin, she typed, **Pass the word, everyone log in NOW. If they need to pee, they should have done it a few minutes ago. LOG IN.**

She already had most of her VR suit on and was settling the headset over her head when she remembered Caspian. "Son of a bitch." She considered, then sent him what she'd planned. **Can you log in without your team knowing? Need to talk details, but in-game.**

The rest of the team was online by the time Caspian logged in.

"Callista?" His voice was uncertain.

"Do they know you're online?" Gracie asked immediately.

"Yes, but not that I'm meeting with you. I said I was going to go wait for you and try to lay some groundwork with the rest of the team so they'd back me up when I suggested a weird team layout later."

"Okay. Any way they're going to see you?"

"There's a chance." Caspian sounded like he was frowning. "But I did the best I could."

"Okay." Gracie shrugged. It was this or nothing. "We're running the Haunt now. Come join us."

"*WHAT?*" He lowered his voice. "What?"

"Come on. Now."

"I wish I'd known to pee."

"Too late," Gracie said unsympathetically. He deserved far more discomfort than a full bladder in her opinion. "We have a limited timeframe."

"Uh…" Caspian waffled, but she heard him heave a sigh a moment later. "Okay, one sec. Let me try something." There was a pause and a scuffling noise, and then he came back. "I told them you have a date tonight, and you'll be online in a few hours. They won't be looking for you for a bit."

"Thanks," Gracie said cautiously. The party invite flashed up from Jay, and she accepted it.

"Can I say something?" Caspian asked her privately.

"Make it quick." She wasn't in a mood for protestations of innocence right now.

Caspian must have sensed that because he broke off in the middle of whatever he had been about to say. "I think we can make it," he told her finally.

"Sure." Gracie had never been one to ice people out before—that was her mother's move—but right now, she was just angry enough to try it. The last thing she wanted to do was be polite to Caspian. Even if he was firmly on their side now, she wasn't sure she'd be able to forgive what he'd done. She didn't need spies and backstabbing in her life.

Still… She sighed.

Despite everything, she just wasn't comfortable punishing people and letting them stew.

"Cas?"

"Yeah?"

"We'll talk about the rest of it later." That was about as nice as she could manage.

"Okay." He sounded relieved. "Um…it may have to be a bit after the run. I'm probably getting fired right after, so I'll have to move out." To her surprise, he was laughing.

"That's funny?"

"I mean, kinda, right?" He was still laughing. "It's ridiculous."

"It really is," Gracie said. A smile was tugging at her mouth. "Okay, fine. Let's do the run, and then we'll, uh, we'll figure out the rest."

"Roger that." He echoed the team's normal terminology easily.

The team loaded into Yesuan's Haunt and skipped the intro. Gracie hated doing that, but they didn't have much time for lore right now. When the aether cleared, though, everyone did take a moment to gasp.

Yesuan had become immortal through his own healing powers, but even he could die by violence—and those who had imprisoned him had wanted him to remember it. Yesuan's Haunt was a fortress, dank and cold. A prison with no windows or balconies, but to reach it, one had to walk across a windy expanse of stone, a single spear that disappeared into utter darkness below. Wind howled around them as they traversed it.

"What is it with these people and heights?" Gracie asked rhetorically.

"One of our team members quit the game after this one," Caspian said. "He dropped out of the run, and then he quit about a week later."

"You're kidding," Alex said, dumbstruck.

"Your old team?" Lakhesis asked, confused.

"Long story," Gracie cut in. "We'll talk about it after. For now, just assume Caspian knows what he's talking about on this run, okay?"

"Okay." Lakhesis sounded like she had a *lot* of questions, but she didn't ask any of them, to Gracie's relief.

The whispers began when they were halfway across the bridge. Screams echoed in the wind, half-heard, half-remembered. Pleading, begging, crying out for mercy.

They had imprisoned him within a wall of his own cruelty. Gracie knew that these were the voices of the people Yesuan had slaughtered, the echoes of his destruction. Gracie could only think that if their goal had been to make Yesuan sane, this hadn't been the best way to do it.

Even she was beginning to wince every time the wind rose. How could she possibly have lasted hundreds of years? Part of her wanted to run, but she squared her shoulders and narrowed her eyes. She had passed all of Harry's tests so far.

She would pass this one too.

CHAPTER TWENTY-FIVE

After the windswept walk, Gracie had expected Yesuan's Haunt to be drafty, filled with the same moaning winds, the castle stones damp and chilled. The sort of place you could never feel comfortable or warm.

Instead, the place was claustrophobic in the extreme. What had looked like a castle in the distance was actually a gigantic hunk of rock, like a piece of a mountain that had been unearthed and then hung precariously on a spire of stone. Runes skittered over the outside of it, clearly shoring up the rock's strength so Yesuan could not break out.

Inside, tunnels had been scraped out of the rock, so small and close that the team had to walk single file. The sounds of their footsteps echoed back at them sharply since there was nowhere for the sound to go.

"Can you imagine being trapped here for centuries?" Dathok asked quietly. "Pacing these hallways, learning every inch of them, and never feeling like you could stand up straight or even take a deep breath?"

No one answered. Their agreement was plain enough in their silent horror, even though their characters' faces were blank.

They weren't far along the corridors when they heard the scream. It was a howl of anguish; not the sort of thing one would hear if someone were being tortured or killed, but the sort of scream that built inside someone until they could not hold it in any longer.

Yesuan. They knew without having to ask. The game had wanted them to feel his captivity before fighting them. That was why they were running through these corridors without fighting anything. They were meant to *feel* the desperation and confinement.

Gracie ran in silence. She was fighting her disdain to understand why Harry had chosen this place for the end of his quest. This was how he saw himself—a superior being, understanding the world in a way no one else could, uniting people against him.

And hated for it. He had turned others' derision and anger into his very *purpose*. Turning it around like a toddler, telling himself that he *wanted* them to hate him. That it was part of some master plan.

He hadn't expected people to like him while he led this world.

In his heart, Harry saw leaders as people who must on some level be despised. He had wanted to bring out the best in everyone else, whether or not he brought out the best in himself.

"What are you thinking about?" To her surprise, it was Caspian who asked the question, not Jay. Jay, she thought, knew her well enough to know that she would tell him when she wanted to share her thoughts. She stole a glance at Anders before answering Caspian. He was walking a few characters back, chainmail glinting dully in the light.

"Thinking about leadership," Gracie told Caspian after a while. "Thinking about whether Yesuan was right."

Caspian made a soft noise, like he was going to protest, but said nothing.

"It's crazy, right?" Gracie asked him. "Doing terrible things, destroying lives to unite people against him—but what if he was right? It makes you wonder. If your goal *isn't* to do bad things or be cruel or hurt people, if your goal is *really* to bring people together, is there a way to ethically do evil things? To serve the greater good and bring people together by being the thing they unite against?"

Caspian, to his credit, actually seemed to think about it. When he spoke again, he sounded pensive. "I imagine you'd hate everyone else in the world if you did that. It doesn't matter if your goal is to do 'good' or not, you're trying to control people. Run them through a maze like a rat. And people are unpredictable, so you end up pitting yourself against them. After a while, I think you'd begin to become evil, no matter how you started."

"Thank you," Gracie said after a moment.

"Huh?" Caspian sounded like he thought she might be setting him up for an insult.

"I know this isn't the real world, but they made this place really convincing," she said softly. "It's enough to make you wonder if you'd do the same thing as Yesuan if you had the chance."

"I don't think any of us will ever have to worry about

that," Caspian replied wryly.

"Mmm."

But he was wrong, and she knew it. Harry had intended to be Yesuan; Gracie was sure of that. That meant that if she passed this final test, she would have the option to become that person in the game. Whatever powers Harry had granted himself—powers meant to control other players—she would have.

Caspian had reminded her not to fall into the same trap Harry had. It was impossible to control people benevolently. Even if she started out playing a part, sooner or later she would find herself believing the role, and embracing it.

In the end, people like Yesuan—like Harry—always ended up in a place like this, reviled and powerless. If she wanted to rule, she would need to find a different path.

The game did not allow her to wallow, however. They heard chittering and maniacal laughter ahead, and Gracie held up a hand to stop the group. Though their enemies could not *hear* them, she still initiated the ready check in silence, and no one spoke while they responded to it. A series of green check marks appeared along the left edge of her screen next to each player's name.

Scuffling sounds let her know that people were changing order, all the melee fighters moving to the front of the group.

Gracie gestured to keep them back and crept along the corridor. From the next bend, she could see torchlight flickering. The laughter was stronger here, as were some of the screams Gracie had heard outside the prison. Frowning, she peered around the bend—and froze in horror.

Oryxa stood at the far end of the cavern. It was impossible to miss her; her naked body shone so pale a gold it was almost white. Long hair blew artfully in a breeze no one else could see, and she walked to and fro as if she knew that everyone's eyes were drawn to her. Gracie shuddered as she looked. Oryxa was truly unsettling, and beautiful in a way that seemed to hint at more.

A moment later, she understood why. Under the perfect mask was a demon who had ruined countless lives, and the character designers had allowed that second form to flicker through. Every once in a while, just for a split-second, you could see the true face behind Oryxa's perfection.

It was horrifying. Blood dripped from long claws, fire lit her flesh from the inside, and her teeth stretched into fangs. The eyes, which were lambent and long-lashed in her human form, were pits of blackness. Imps tumbled around her, fire trailing in their wake.

"Oryxa shouldn't pull until we've cleared the room," Gracie said to the group, "but I don't see any barrier for the boss fight the way there would normally be. We know that they patched this instance, so everyone be on your toes. Stay as far back as you can, and send out a team alert if you think Oryxa has aggroed."

A yes came back in a chorus.

"*If she pulls,*" Gracie said, her mind racing, "Lakhesis, I want you to main-tank her for the first little bit. Do you feel okay with that?"

"Sure," Lakhesis said.

"I'll use AoE to grab the rest of the room, and Ushanas, Freon, and Fys, you'll use *your* AoE to burn them down as quickly as possible. Caspian, you'll keep Lakhesis alive, and

Lakhesis, you'll kite Oryxa at the end of the room until we have the rest of the mobs killed."

"Got it," Lakhesis replied at the same time Caspian agreed, "Will do." They both sounded resolute.

"Pulling the first group now," Gracie said. She waited for the rest of the melee team to approach and fan out nearby, then she used a shield-throw to get an imp's attention.

Its head whipped around, and it and its two companions came hopping toward her at high speed, already throwing fireballs. Gracie stood firm as they approached, then ran a few yards out to meet them, slamming her fist on the ground to do damage to all of them. With their attention firmly fixed on her, she chose one and began to focus on it in particular. The melee group followed suit, and when it reached ten percent health, she switched to her next target so that she could keep its attention focused on her when they began hitting it as well.

If Caspian hadn't given her a heads-up, she would never have known that Yesuan's Haunt had changed, but with the warning, she could see the faint signs of it. The imps and incubi, which should be relatively quick to kill, took a bit longer than usual, and Gracie could see that her team members were getting critical hits less often than they usually would.

She felt a grudging respect for Dan and Dhruv. They knew how little it would take to make an instance too difficult, and they had done a good job of being subtle.

They were halfway across the room when Oryxa

noticed them, and Gracie swore internally. She had been hoping against hope that they weren't going to change a boss fight that way, but they had.

She allowed herself one moment to wonder if they would even make it to Yesuan, then shook her head angrily and focused her attention on the trash mobs around her. She'd be damned if she let them take her down this early in the fight.

She was going to fucking *win*.

"I'm on her!" Lakhesis called. "Cas?"

"I've gotcha," Caspian called back. He was circling the edge of the room, out of the range of the trash mobs Gracie was taking on. "Kite away."

"Here." Freon sent an ice spear at Oryxa. "Let me know if you want any more of those, okay? It'll help you kite."

Gracie smiled. She was in the middle of a huge group of trash mobs now and Alan was barely able to keep up with the healing, but it was awesome to see her team improvising and helping one another on the fly.

She lost herself in the mechanics of surviving the fight, only tracking Lakhesis and Caspian via their voices. They were laughing, which let her know that things weren't going too crazy, so Gracie took a moment to heal back to full health when she finished her cleanup of the room.

"Alan, you good for the boss fight?"

"As good as I will be." Alan, thankfully, sounded amused. "Go for it."

"Awesome. Caspian, find the other healers, and Lakhesis, you've got backup!"

"Woot!" Lakhesis sounded amused. "Glad someone else

is here to give this bitch a piece of their mind. She keeps turning into a bloody zombie while she chases me, and it's freaking me the fuck out."

Gracie snorted. "You didn't find it even a *little* worrisome to have a naked supermodel trying to kill you?" She reached Oryxa and threw her shield, sending the beautiful woman staggering sideways and whipping around to face her. "'Sup, bitch? Heard you want to destroy the world." She saw the flash of Oryxa's true form. "Oh, *crap*, that's terrifying."

"Yeah, and the rest of the time she's so pretty and sweet that it feels like she's probably right to kill you." Lakhesis was laughing. "Wait 'til she starts talking. She has this melodious voice, telling you to rest a while and come closer like she hasn't even noticed you're trying to kill her —then *bam*, zombie crazy-eyes."

"Young men, take note," Alan said wryly. "A pretty face can hide a *lot* of crazy." He laid down a group heal. "Gracie, be careful. That poison effect she has is pretty nasty."

"Thanks," Gracie called back.

"The crazy thing goes for dudes, too," Kevin chimed in. His amarok leapt at Oryxa and slashed with its claws.

"*Agreed*," chorused Gracie, Lakhesis, and Ushanas.

"Why must we fight?" Oryxa asked, her voice echoing through the room. "Stay a while, and let me make the hurt go away."

"Creepy," Gracie said.

"Come, let me tend to your wounds." Oryxa stretched out long, pale fingers, an eerie smile playing around her lips. There was a flash of darkness in her eyes, and then it was gone again, and there was only her unsettling beauty.

Gracie didn't answer. She was surprised to find herself responding to Oryxa, feeling the fury and annoyance she always felt around women who were beautifully made up. Oryxa was better than she was, part of her mind said. Oryxa was ladylike and polite, and Gracie was a sweaty mess with straggly hair and a dirty face. She was thirteen again, trying to figure out which shade of lipstick to wear while her crushes drooled after her older sister.

Goddammit.

Oryxa's flashes of her true form were becoming more frequent, however.

"Do you think you can save him?" she hissed, and her voice was now hoarser. "He thought he was using us, but we've had centuries to turn him into one of our own. There is no light left in him."

Gracie felt a chill. She had wondered why Oryxa would ally herself with someone whose true goal had been to create goodness and light in the world, and now she understood. Oryxa had known that over the centuries, Yesuan's heart would become dark and twisted. She had hoped that when he broke out, he would become an agent of the demons.

How many sweet, twisted words had Oryxa murmured in Yesuan's ears over the years? She was immortal so she could play the long game.

"You're nothing," Gracie told her. "You thrive off the pain mortals cause each other. You stoke the fire, but you're nothing on your own, and when your cruelty doesn't take root, you die."

She swept her sword down in an angled stroke, and Oryxa stumbled back. The beautiful mask flickered again.

"You're *nothing*," Gracie told her again.

"*You'll never turn him!*" Oryxa's shriek was furious. "You'll have to destroy him."

This, Gracie realized, was the true cruelty of Oryxa. The player came to Yesuan's Haunt, thinking that they would kill him, and Oryxa reminded them that they had not even tried to save him first.

She reminded them, before they faced him, that they were powerless to make him sane and good again.

Gracie shuddered and clamped her lips shut. She was not going to let Oryxa taunt her. This was not her failure. Yesuan had willingly plunged himself into darkness, and Oryxa had spent centuries—millennia—making him more twisted.

Whatever Yesuan had once been, he was not that any longer.

Whatever Harry had created, whatever he had dreamed, he was now standing in its way.

Gracie stepped forward with a last yell, driving her sword through Oryxa's body. The succubus gave a scream that made Gracie's teeth vibrate and her mask crumbled, leaving only her anger and cruelty on display as she writhed and died.

Gracie stood over her, panting. The amarok was at her side, and Jay, and Dathok. When she looked over her shoulder, the rest of the team was standing quietly. Normally, they would be cheering, but it was clear that Oryxa's taunts had unnerved them.

"We have to keep moving," Gracie told them. "I don't know how long we've got, but if they find out we're making this run, they may pull the servers down. We have to get to Yesuan. Come on."

Sam watched out of the corner of his eye as Dan checked his phone for what had to be about the twentieth time in five minutes. Dan was getting nervous, as if he knew something was up.

It was time to send in the second round of distractions.

Sam nodded to the newbie, a kid fresh out of high school, who had passed the entrance test with flying colors and was eager to prove himself. Although he was very young in some ways, he'd been a model employee, and it was impossible to hate him.

Or be rude to him.

"Hey, Laurie."

"Hi." The kid came bounding over. "You need anything, boss?"

"No, no," Sam assured him. "I just realized, though—didn't you used to play disc golf?"

"Yeah!" Laurie lit up. With his round face and curls, he looked faintly cherubic. Sam wondered when he'd gotten old enough that people under the age of twenty-five looked like babies to him.

"You know, Dhruv also played disc golf," Sam said off-handedly. "I know he thought about starting a company team for a while."

"Really?" Laurie looked around to where Dhruv was leaning against a wall, eating a piece of pizza and staring into space. "Do you think I should… Do you think he'd mind if I…"

"No, he likes hearing from employees," Sam assured him. "Go on, talk to him."

He watched while Laurie headed over to Dhruv and started chatting excitedly. Dhruv, despite himself, was taken in, and Sam headed over to Dan. This was the more complicated part of the plan. He nodded to the seat beside Dan. "Do you have a sec? I wanted to talk to you about something."

Dan was too much of a professional to do anything except nod. He gave Sam a bland look. "What's on your mind?"

"Have you talked to Jay at all?" Sam asked. He saw Dan's face become guarded. This was a risky plan, but Sam knew that nothing was more interesting to Dan right now than the issue of Callista. Talking about some non-core piece of it might just be the only thing that would distract Dan from going to check on the servers manually.

"I haven't," Dan said after a moment. "I know you want there to be good feeling, Sam, but I hope you understand. Sometimes in these situations, there simply isn't any way to make everybody happy."

"No, no, I get that." Sam forced a smile. "I just thought… well, Jay was popular on this team. They miss him, and I think maybe if you were to talk to him, explain how unusual this situation is, you'd feel comfortable letting him come back. They'd all feel better, and you wouldn't have to worry about an early employee being on the loose. Our non-compete isn't super-strong, after all."

Dan considered this. "Huh," he said after a moment.

Sam made a little internal prayer: *Come on, Jay, keep this thing rolling. I don't know how long I've got.* Out loud, he said, "Obviously, you'd want to make sure there were strict rules in place for how he spoke to the team about what happened."

Just a little longer. He just had to keep Dan occupied for a little longer.

CHAPTER TWENTY-SIX

The trash mobs between Oryxa and Yesuan were meant to be much easier than the first set. The closer they got, the more skeletons and shattered shards of rock lay scattered around the floor. Yesuan had begun to go insane, and he was killing his allies.

Gracie wondered if Oryxa had known about *that*.

The patch on this instance, however, meant that the remaining mobs were just a *little* stronger than they should have been. Once or twice, new groups came at quicker intervals than they should have, and the group had very nearly had some deaths. While they *could* battle-resurrect in this instance, it was a mana-intensive spell that meant either Alan or Caspian would have to take time off from healing.

They made it through, however, by burning a truly insane number of potions. By the time they reached the innermost sanctuary, they still had a respectable amount of time on the dungeon timer and most of the group's cooldown abilities were ready to go.

"Any last pieces of advice?" Gracie asked Caspian publicly.

"I expect you know what Lirael and Azrael are susceptible to," Caspian said. He waited for the nod. "And to burn them down before you go to Yesuan, right? And the counter on his interrupt? Yep, nothing other than those. You have to stay on-point for the fight, but it's not anything super-complex."

Gracie nodded. "Anyone have questions?"

Everyone shook their heads.

"I think we should go now," Lakhesis said. She emoted a smile and a flex at Gracie. "If they're trying to slow us down, we need to take every minute we have available, right?"

"Yep." Gracie smiled back. "Let's go kick some asses. And if anything goes haywire, just keep your wits about you and help out where people need it, okay? I have no idea what might be unusual about this fight."

Everyone laughed, but they were already focused on the fight. The ready check only took a couple of seconds, and then they were streaming across the barrier and fanning out, everyone giving Gracie an air high-five as they went past.

Caspian alone did not. Instead, he bowed. She heard him draw breath to speak—

A muffled voice came across his line, and it wasn't his. Caspian said something and there was a sudden argument, escalating quickly. Caspian's voice was rising, as was the voice of the person he was arguing with.

"Not a big deal," Gracie heard. "Just a practice run. She's not even—okay, fine. No. Look, I'll hold them up. Just go get Evan. Look, seriously, I have it under control. What's such a big deal about this?"

Everyone in the game exchanged glances. Caspian was frozen, not yet over the barrier, and the timer on the boss fight had started ticking. Thirty more seconds and he'd be locked out.

"Caspian," Gracie said sharply. "You need to get in here. Wrap that up, whatever it is."

Caspian said something indecipherable, and a door slammed in the background. His character ran over the barrier and Gracie followed.

"What's going on?" she asked him bluntly.

"Thad found me," Caspian said. His voice was grim. "I told them you weren't around this evening, so they didn't need to be checking the servers, and I'd just be questing. I don't know why he came to find me, but he saw where we were."

Dread settled into the pit of Gracie's stomach. "So…"

"So we need to kill this guy *quick*," Caspian said. "Because they're going to tell Dragon Soul we're here."

"You heard him," Gracie told the team. "Everybody move. Give me twenty good minutes, no mistakes. You can do this. I know you guys have it in you."

"Drag Lirael to the right and Azrael to the left," Caspian said suddenly. "I just remembered—we noticed it all works better when you do that. No idea why. Might just be a coincidence, but—"

"We'll take anything we can get," Gracie said. "Lakhesis, you go for Lirael. I'll take Azrael. Alan, Caspian, you be ready with your corrupts on Azrael, and Ushanas, you go all hellfire and brimstone on Lirael. Boost your power as much as you can right now. Whatever potions you have, burn 'em. It does us no good to get through those two unscathed if they take the servers down. *GO!*"

The team scattered. Lakhesis darted to the left around Yesuan, grabbing Lirael and pulling her to the right, and Gracie did the opposite with Azrael.

"*YOU THINK TO JUDGE ME?*" Yesuan yelled. "*YOU HAVE SEEN NOTHING, AND YOU KNOW NOTHING. I HAVE SEEN THE FACE OF DEATH.*"

"Woof," Dathok muttered.

"Yeah, this guy has no chill," Caspian said, with a laugh. "He's—"

"*YOUR SPELLS HAVE NO POWER HERE!*" Yesuan yelled. An AoE spell interrupt followed, breaking the mages' larger spells.

"That's one," Kevin called. "He's going quick, so be ready to scatter when you need to, okay?"

Everyone agreed. Lakhesis was already back in motion, and Gracie could dimly hear the sound of fiery arrows rushing overhead and fireballs striking the ground. Ushanas was not about to let anyone survive her firestorm.

Azrael, meanwhile, was snarling his rage as he clawed at Gracie. Unlike Oryxa, his angelic appearance was real… in a way. Azrael *had* been an angel, one of the few who had been tasked with creating the Aosi. He had been unwilling to let go of the idea that the Aosi were the chosen ones, and he had joined Yesuan in his exile.

He had become just as crazy as Yesuan, it seemed.

"You lack the will to triumph!" His words were a hiss. "Yesuan alone sees what must be done."

"Yeah, yeah." Gracie kept burning him down as Caspian

and Alan stacked corrupts on him. "Just die already, would you? I don't have time for this shit. Lakhesis, how's it going?"

"She's on fire," Lakhesis called back. "Going slowly. Maybe a third left?"

Gracie didn't respond. Azrael was twisting, clawing, and growing. His skin flickered gray-green, showing the rot inside him. He had been unearthly before, his skin deep blue, as luminous as the night sky, and his eyes like stars.

But the evil he had been exposed to had begun to decay him from the inside out. His night-black hair was turning brittle, graying and falling from his head as the fight progressed.

"*YOUR SPELLS HAVE NO POWER HERE!*" Yesuan yelled, and Gracie blinked, trying to remember if—

"*SCATTER!*" Kevin called. "*NOW!*"

Everyone ran. No one had a plan, they just ran.

It was good, though, because the stun and damage spells came quickly, one after the other.

"Now, back in!" Kevin yelled. "But keep listening. Harry's in there now, and he's going to do whatever he can to fuck with us."

"Shitballs," Gracie muttered. "Is that why we scattered after two instead of three?"

"Yeah. I saw him moving differently."

"Good looking out." She gave him a feral grin and swung her arm to send her shield flying toward Azrael. "Just one lucky crit and I'll be…dammit." She charged him and brought one arm up to catch her shield before slamming it sideways into his body, and followed that slam up with a slash of her sword. Azrael went rigid, then his body collapsed. Some streamed up into nothingness like stars in the night, and the rest crumbled to the floor like rotten leaves.

"Ew," Alan muttered. "Seriously, *ew*."

"One—more—fireball—" Ushanas called from between gritted teeth, and a moment later there was a series of whoops from their team. "Lirael's down!"

"Scatter again!" Kevin called.

Everyone ran like hell, and Gracie knew she had only just made it out of the way when the stun went off again, followed by a wave of damage that would have killed any of them.

"Back in," she called. "Don't let him cut me off from the group this time. We fight together, and that's how we'll win." She already had her character running for Yesuan. "Hi, Harry," she said as she launched her shield forward in a stun. Yesuan staggered back. "Fancy seeing you here."

CHAPTER TWENTY-SEVEN

Evan was on a conference call when Thad burst into his office.

"They're in Yesuan's Haunt," Thad said. Evan frowned at him, and Thad resisted the urge to growl. "You know how we had that conference call? They just went in. Jamie's trying to slow them down, but…"

His voice trailed off.

"But?" Evan asked. "Look, how much time do we have before—"

"Son of a *bitch*," Thad said quietly.

He recognized the scenery behind Jamie's character. They were already *at* Yesuan. That meant they'd been in the instance for a while, and *that* meant that when Jamie had told them Callista wouldn't be online that night…

He must already have known that she was planning to run the instance.

Fury came in a rush, and he left the room at high speed. Evan called after him, but Thad didn't care. He jumped most of the way down a half-flight of stairs in the stairwell and barely recovered in time to keep from wiping out. He didn't even notice the rush of adrenaline, he was so infuriated.

He reached the small solo playing room within a minute, heedless of the stares he was getting from the rest of them, and put his shoulder into it as he turned the handle. He might tackle Jamie sideways, but the man deserved it.

Unfortunately, Jamie had thought of that. The door shuddered but didn't open.

He'd locked himself in.

"JAMIE!" Thad yelled. He pounded on the door.

There was no answer.

"Sooooo, they definitely know what we're doing," Caspian reported. "Also, not super-important, but I am all kinds of fired."

"Join the club," Jay said with amusement.

"Focus," Gracie said. "We're on the clock."

"Yes, ma'am." Jay sounded like he was laughing.

Harry watched them approach. There was no mistaking that a person was controlling this character, and Gracie wondered savagely if he was enjoying *being* Yesuan, as he'd always imagined himself to be.

"Too afraid to fight me alone?" he called to her. "Too much of a coward?"

Gracie only smiled. *If you believe you're going to use some outdated notion of chivalry to make me do stupid things, you're very much mistaken,* she thought. She said nothing, however. She didn't want to give Harry anything to work with.

This wasn't a normal fight, and that gave her considerable freedom. She had some stuns in her rotation, and some high-damage strikes. Normally, she wouldn't use those in a fight like this, concentrating instead on attacks that generated threat and kept her enemies focused on her.

But with Harry in the other position, threat was useless.

No force of habit, Gracie told herself sternly. *You told them to give you twenty minutes with no slip-ups, so you give them the same.*

That steadied her. She had never liked reacting, pushing back. It meant the other person controlled the fight and the direction. But she realized that she *did* like doing her best for a team to lift *everyone* up.

That was the part Harry didn't understand. He viewed leadership the same way Yesuan did: him against the world. That was why he'd written the character. He didn't understand that a leader, like everyone else, needed to strive to be their best self, inspired by the ones they led.

Gracie charged, feinted to the left, and sent her character into a roll the other way, feeling a shudder through her haptics as Yesuan's staff thudded on the floor.

"Everybody out of range!" she called.

The spellcasters had already been at their farthest range, so it was only the melee team that needed to run. Gracie watched them scatter, and she was just out of range when the stun came, followed immediately by the heavy-damage strike. Harry wasn't going to play by Yesuan's rules. He was going to use these abilities as often as he could and destroy them.

Alex gave a yell, and Gracie turned to see Teef stretched out on the ground, dead. The panther hadn't been able to escape quickly enough.

Oh, *hell* no. You killed pets, you were a hundred percent the scum of the earth. That was Gracie's rule.

"For Teef!" she called as she charged back in. "Jay, let's have some fun."

Jay gave a yell of agreement. "For Teef!"

"Everyone, go hard frost!" Gracie called.

Alex was the first one to take up the challenge, switching to frost enchants on his arrows and beginning a heavy damage rotation. Gracie could sense his fury radiating through the room. Teef wasn't "real," but Alex also hated anyone who hurt animals.

With Kevin, Freon, and Lakhesis added to the mix, Harry was suddenly snared and slowed without respite. The team settled into a rhythm quickly, calling out to one another. Kevin would send a smaller freeze and the amarok would dart in with complementary damage, then Alex would loose an ice volley, Lakhesis would use her freezing stun, and Freon would finish with an ice spear. When they were done, Gracie used her own stun, taking deep pleasure in the feel of her fist striking the carpeted floor of her living room.

It occurred to her that her downstairs neighbors probably despised her and Alex.

Oops.

"You think you can win?" Harry shouted. "You're starlings, scavengers, attacking the better fighter."

"You're an asshole," Jay called back, "who wants everything to be his way or the highway. And you know what? If you weren't such an asshole, you'd have a team at your back, too."

Gracie gave a small smile and spun, ducking as she did so to slide under a bolt of holy magic from Yesuan's staff. Everything about him was corrupted, dark magic playing around the light, woven through it.

You could only pretend to be evil for so long. Then the mask became your true face.

The melee team began scattering, and Gracie realized a moment later that Kevin must be telling them individually to leave. She caught his wave and headed out with a nod, hearing Harry's shriek of anger.

He had the strike ready to go now, which put them in a strange position. The moment anyone came in close, he'd kill them.

Gracie knew what had to happen, but it was a risky game. They only got so many chances.

"Everyone, get your strongest strike ready," she said quietly. "Dathok, you're going to try to get his attention, and Lakhesis is going to sneak in behind. She'll stun if she can, and you get off the strongest strike you can. Lakhesis, you try to get out. He might kill both of you, though. Everyone else, as soon as he's loosed the AoE, get in and burn him as much as you can."

Dathok ran in, Jay accompanying him until they were close to Harry. Both of them dodged in and then circled out, staying in front of him so that if he swiveled, he might not see Lakhesis.

When her stun went off, Jay peeled off, and Dathok and Lakhesis darted into range for their strongest strikes. They were burning Harry down as quickly as they could, and

Lakhesis scattered out of range again before Harry could recover and use his own stun.

Dathok wasn't so lucky. As the sacrificial lamb, his health bar plunged to zero a moment later, and there was a heavy sigh down the line.

"Good man," Gracie said. "Everyone else, avenge the fallen."

There was a roar of agreement, and ice and fire came rushing past Gracie. The remaining melee team charged, and Harry staggered sideways, trying to get off spells as stun after stun stopped him.

"Stuns are done in two seconds," Lakhesis warned, and Gracie waited for the others to run as she wound up her own shield bash.

Just one more second…one more…

She swung her arm to send the shield flying at Harry's face, and he staggered back with a yell. With the shield out of her hands and circling around, Gracie gave a two-handed slash with her sword, then returned it to her left hand, and grabbed her shield in her right as she ran out of range.

This time, they needed to use more than one distraction to get inside Harry's range. Kevin's amarok ran forward with Chowder, while Lakhesis snuck up behind, and when Harry turned on Lakhesis with a roar, Gracie charged at his now-turned back to stun him.

A few moments of furious strikes and they ran, Lakhesis sending a parting stun so the mages could dart into range for a few fireballs.

Harry was at a quarter health, and hardly able to get a single one of his spells off. He should be dead, Gracie thought—but Dragon Soul had done their work well with this patch. Harry was hanging on, stronger than he would normally be.

If this was how they wanted to play, she'd do it.

They just didn't have much time. She could practically *feel* their attention turning towards the servers, the Dragon Soul founders running for that room—

"Give it everything you've got!" she called. "Jay—" *It has to be you.*

He looked across the group to give her a nod. Gracie couldn't die in this fight, so he would do it without question. He charged, and when Harry waited, sure Jay would dart out of range again, Jay just kept running.

Harry had swiveled, sure this was part of a group effort, so Jay got in three heavy strikes before Harry was able to stun and kill him. Jay's health bar plunged, and his character sprawled to the ground.

Gracie yelled in fury. It wasn't real, she knew, but she had felt her heart twist when Jay's character fell. He was lying near Dathok's body and Teef's, and Harry was trying to tear the whole team down so Gracie would be alone.

Like he was.

"*Everyone!*" she shouted. She didn't need to, because they were already in motion. Alex had switched from ice to fire, taking advantage of the higher damage, and the other team members followed suit. It was risky—they had this chance, and no more—but they knew that the longer they delayed, the higher the chance the servers would go down.

Harry screamed his anger. "You're a coward!"

"And you're an asshole." Gracie used Jay's words. "You know," she called to him, as she threw her shield away and launched into the fight with two-handed strikes, "I felt sorry for you. I wondered if you were right. But all you wanted was to control people—and the story you wrote here, what happened to Yesuan? It's what would happen to you, too."

Harry snarled his fury at her. "You don't have the first idea what it means to rule."

"No, I don't," Gracie agreed. The others had stepped back to let her finish this herself, and she shook her head. "Don't give him any chances, guys! I don't care who gets the killing strike."

They began burning him down. Five percent, four, three—

"You're right," Gracie told Harry. "I don't know what it means to rule, but I know what it means to lead."

Whoever fired the killing shot, Harry staggered and dropped to the ground.

"And that's better," Gracie said. "Because it means I'm here with my team. I have people who back me up, and we go farther than you ever would have on your own. If you only want to rule—"

The world went black, the servers down at last.

Too late, Gracie thought with satisfaction.

"If you only want to rule," she finished, taking off her helmet in the stillness of her living room, "you've stopped viewing humans as people—and that means you're not fit to lead them."

Dan stared at the servers, his heart pounding. The message

had come in on his phone and he had run—*sprinted*—for the server rooms, fury and disbelief coursing through him.

Had he made it in time? Had he—

His phone buzzed.

Game mode activated, the message title read. He opened the email with shaking fingers. It took two tries, and when he saw the email, his shoulders slumped.

The Forgotten King Returns.

To his surprise, what was bubbling up in his chest was laughter. Harry had planned this meticulously, to the point of a taunting email when the quest was finished. Only, it wasn't Harry who'd won. Dan hadn't been watching, but deep down, he knew Harry had been outflanked.

"Not the Forgotten King returning," he said out loud. "The new queen rising."

The door opened, and Thad practically fell into the practice room.

"Hello," Jamie said equably.

"What. The *hell*?" Thad said through gritted teeth.

"Funny thing," Jamie said, his tone bland. "The more you see of her, the better you understand why she wins."

"She won because you helped her!" Thad yelled back.

"Yeah," Jamie said. "So ask yourself why I didn't help you instead?" He slipped past Thad and tossed a glance over his shoulder. "I'll clean out my room and be gone by this afternoon. And you can all go back to doing all the backstabby bullshit you didn't grow out of in the fourth grade."

Gracie's phone was buzzing, vibrating against her arm as she wrapped her arms around Alex and hugged him tightly.

"You should get that," he said.

"Nah, it's just Harry."

"Okay, but counterpoint: you're crushing my ribs. Good Lord, woman, you're a *menace* when you work out."

Gracie let go of him with a laugh and looked at her phone. Harry's number. She gave a sigh and a shrug. "I'm not answering that," she said.

"You know what you should do," Alex said, "since the servers are down?"

"What?" Gracie went to the fridge and grabbed two beers. She peered around the doorway of the kitchen as she popped the caps and brought Alex a bottle.

"You should talk to Jay," Alex said, taking a sip.

Gracie choked on her beer. "I, uh…maybe."

"Maybe? Now, where's the Gracie who took matters into her own hands and gave Sydney my number? Could it be that she's perfectly happy to push *other* people into relationships, but she's… Oh, what's the term I'm looking for?"

"Stop it!" Gracie shoved him, laughing.

"A total coward," Alex said. "Harry was right, you know. He just had the context wrong."

"Asshole." Gracie was laughing, though.

"No," Alex said. "No, *this* is the asshole move: you call Jay and get things moving or I'll drop a bomb, just like you did with Sydney."

"*No.*" Gracie gave him a pleading look. "No. You wouldn't."

Alex leaned forward until his nose was an inch from hers. "*Try me!*"

"Oh, shit. I know that expression." Gracie tipped her head back and drank as much of the beer as she could in one sip. "Oh, maybe that was a bad choice. Now I'm going to be tipsy. Crap."

"Best get it out of the way before the alcohol hits, then," Alex said blandly.

"Fuck you. Okay, *fine.* But go to your room, I don't want you listening." Gracie put the beer down, smoothed her suddenly sweaty palms on her pants, and opened her laptop. Her stomach flip-flopped when she saw that Jay was online, and she pressed the video call button with shaking fingers.

One battle at a time. And it was time for this one.

The story continues in book three, Reign With Axe And Shield, available now at Amazon and through Kindle Unlimited.

No one wanted Gracie to become the Queen - hell, *Gracie* didn't want to be the Queen.

She is, though, and people are just lining up to take shots at her. Some want her gone, some want what she has…

…And one of them is determined to destroy the entire game if he can't get what he wants.

Which means that Gracie might just have to team up with the absolute last people she wanted to: Dan and Dhruv.

Her only consolation? They hate the idea, too.

Click here to get your copy today.

AUTHOR NOTES - NATALIE GREY

APRIL 12, 2019

Thank you for reading the Metamorphosis Online series! As someone who has found solace, courage, and inspiration in video games, this series is near and dear to my heart. Playing and writing video games has been a transformative experience in storytelling for me, and I count myself very lucky to have these stories as part of my life.

One of the things I love about working with Michael is that he pushes me to step beyond myself and trust my instincts. From his first concepts of Gracie and the world, I felt both very inspired…and somewhat as if I'd been thrown in the deep end of a pool. Working together to bring the world to life has been incredibly fun, a challenge every day to bring my A game to match Michael's. I am so lucky to be able to work with him.

I want to thank the whole team at LMBPN—the incredible editorial staff, Jay (who designed these amazing covers), Steve, and all of the people behind the scenes who I haven't met, but have helped bring my books into the world. I also want to thank the team at Abyssal Arts for giving me my first opportunity to write a video game, the readers whose appreciation pushed me to find new and better stories (as well as new and better ways of telling them), and B and L, who inspire me to be my best self every day, in everything I do.

I can't wait to bring you more of this world, and new worlds!

Sincerely,
Nat

THANK YOU for not only reading this story but these *Author Notes* as well.

(I think I've been good with always opening with "thank you." If not, I need to edit the other *Author Notes*!)

RANDOM (*sometimes*) THOUGHTS?

<THIS IS A BIT OF A RANT—FEEL FREE TO SKIP IT!>

Right now, I'm working out the blurb for this book, and this story has me a bit melancholy.

Why? *I'm glad you asked.*

Many of LMBPN's stories (like one series about a Witch, the FBI, and friends in school) are pretty straightforward. The challenges and prospects might concern relationships, but they are often just a handful in quantity.

In this series, the concepts in question (I am guessing) have been a concern for MMORPG creators for years.

If a human does something with no consequences, will

that change them? If they are allowed to live out being an ugly asshole, will they act this way in real life?

OR

What if they live out being courageous in the game? Will that change them in real life? Will they grow a backbone and stand up for their rights?

I think the answer to both of these questions is the same. If something about the game changes a person, it would change some people in good ways, and some people in bad ways.

However, there is nothing to say that bad people won't find another conduit to encourage them to do bad things. If we want to limit the societal impact, you would need to shut down the Internet, cut off television, and limit books.

Even then you would have some go nuts.

So, instead of dreaming up reasons that MMORPG games can hurt people, how about figuring out if the risk is any greater than the other forms of input which feeds a person's thoughts.

I'm against randomly shutting stuff down, but I'm a realist as well. With the latest news coming out that a man planned to become a copycat terrorist and rent a moving truck and run over people, it proves that delivering examples will affect people.

So what? How about we hold people to account for their actions, and realize that the decisions we choose now will affect the world in a hundred years?

What will be our population at that time? Assuming we don't have a post-apocalyptic event, it's going to be a metric buttload.

We have the technology to feed everyone; we just need

to do it. We have the nascent abilities to create housing with 3D printers. Start paying to implement it.

Hell, I'm curious what it would take to build a few houses. Let's start it in countries where a good-enough home is a hundred times better than the home they have now. I've been blessed to travel the world, and I'm very aware of the homes some live in now.

I live in the United States of America, and I am very aware of the quality of some homes. In a couple of words, THEY SUCK.

There are a ton of reasons that providing homes here in the USA is stupidly expensive, and they start with regulations / codes / laws about building houses.

However, before someone points out the regulations are the reasons for it being expensive to build, I'd like to ask just WHO the jack-wipes were who did such piss-poor jobs of building homes that we needed a big book of rules in the first place?

Unfortunately, we have self-centered people so focused on themselves that they are incapable of considering the benefits to others over themselves. It isn't until someone 'makes' them do the right thing (which they bitch about) that they perhaps realize it was their effort to screw someone that put the law in place.

And they will only care because now there are rules / laws / certifications which they must abide by, and it makes their days more difficult.

In other countries, the regulations can be ignored by greasing some palms. This only works if the building doesn't fall down. When that happens, the government looks for the culprits, and sometimes, lines them up in front of a firing squad.

I would love to have a chance to use a virtual world and try out our new technology (food, housing, etc.)

I bet you with ten million freaking gamers and the right game, we would fix the world's fucking problems inside ten years.

Give enough young people a few stats, a sword, and a way to level up by feeding people, and get the hell out of the way.

I might be a realist, but I'm ALL the way an optimist.

Now, go play something and SMITE THE SHIT OUT OF IT!

(Editor's note: And THIS is why we love ya!)

<RANT ENDED>

AROUND THE WORLD IN 80 DAYS

One of the interesting (at least to me) aspects of my life is the ability to work from anywhere and at any time. In the future, I hope to re-read my own *Author Notes* and remember my life as a diary entry.

Inside a metal tube flying over the Sea of Cortez heading to San José del Cabo

Not much to say. I've been reading this book, working on the *Author Notes*, and heading towards the blurb. The mountainous region of Baja California shows me we have plenty of land. We just need to figure out how to engineer and use it.

I'm heading to rest for a week (I hope) and take it easy. I plan on reading five to ten books and have a stupidly glorious grin on my face when I fly back to LAX.

Peace, fellow readers. I'm outta here...

;-)

FAN PRICING

$0.99 Saturdays (new LMBPN stuff) and $0.99 Wednesday (both LMBPN books and friends of LMBPN books.) Get great stuff from us and others at tantalizing prices.

Go ahead. I bet you can't read just one.

Sign up here: http://lmbpn.com/email/.

HOW TO MARKET FOR BOOKS YOU LOVE

Review them so others have your thoughts, and tell friends and the dogs of your enemies (because who wants to talk to enemies?)... *Enough said ;-)*

Ad Aeternitatem,

Michael Anderle

Initiate

It was just one fight, but it changed Kaiden Jericho's life forever.

He was in a gang but was trying to change his future when a board member of the elite advanced academy NEXUS made a snap decision and offered him a chance.

Then fate, or an unbalanced genius, offered him another.

The Nexus Academy is for the elite trainees from Earth, and now trials from our alien allies, as they teach the future generation how to fight, lead, hack, spy, and many other talents and tactics.

Hired by companies, governments and NGOs, these graduates work to pay off the massive debt their training at the academy accumulates.

You don't become the best of the best by staying alive. With the Animus, you are closer to perfection with each death you suffer.

Kaiden Jericho would rather skip the death part, thank you very much.

Initiate is available now at Amazon.com

Death Becomes Her

What you thought you knew about Vampires and Werewolves is wrong...so very, very, wrong.

A thousand years of effort to keep the UnknownWorld hidden is unraveling and the Patriarch is tired. He needs to find someone to take over.

He finds Bethany Anne.

Unknown, untested and untried she sets out to accomplish the impossible while forging a new future. One that no one knew was in danger.

And she does it with an attitude that will make you stand up and cheer!

They say a dress can make a woman, but in this case, the dress is Death, and *Death Becomes Her very well indeed.*

Start the series that launched the Kurtherian Gambit Universe today at Amazon.com

Feared By Hell

You never mess with a young girl around James Brownstone.

The world has changed since the news of Oriceran came out twenty years before. Now, countries all over the world have agreed to using a bounty system for dangerous criminals using advanced magic or advanced technology.

People too powerful for the cops to deal with.

Magical criminals, thugs and bounty hunters, in the future *we revert to what worked in the past.*

if you find out you are hunted by Brownstone, we suggest you turn yourself in.

It will save you a monumental ass-kicking.

Brownstone likes his life simple, but Life is about to throw him a wicked curveball.

Get book one of the Unbelievable Mr. Brownstone series from Amazon today.

Mahalia